THE

POISONED GENIUS

A Thriller of Science, Deceit, and Dark Secrets

ECHO SABLE

TABLE OF CONTENTS

CHAPTER I

PASSING OF A SCIENTIFIC GIANT

In the dim light of my study, the telegram glowed with an urgency that defied its age. My eyes scanned its terse lines thrice, each time my disbelief growing. The request was straightforward, almost mundane, but its implications were anything but.

"Mr. Ash Morris, we are eager for your presence in Vienna. We face a perplexing problem that only your expertise, as recommended by Dr. Tanaka Maisaichi, can resolve. If you choose to assist us, please inform us at your earliest convenience. Sincerely, the Vienna Scientists Association."

Vienna—across the ocean from my quiet abode—was renowned as a bastion of intellectual fervor. Just as it was the capital of music, it stood as the epicenter of scientific innovation.

When it came to Dr. Tanaka Maisaichi, our encounters had been fleeting. Despite his distinct Japanese presence, there wasn't enough familiarity to justify an unexpected invitation that spanned continents.

The telegram had thrown me off balance. An acquaintance barely known, accompanied by a cadre of unknown scientists, had summoned me so abruptly, so unexpectedly.

I sighed deeply, pondering the absurdity of the situation. The allure of mystery tugged at my curiosity, yet the prospect of entertaining every whimsical telegram was exhausting.

Determined to decline, I reached for paper to draft a polite refusal. Just then, Flora, my wife, entered with her characteristic briskness. Before I could speak, she queried, "Do you know the members of the Vienna Scientists Association?"

I chuckled, "You've done your homework, haven't you? But it's not hard to imagine they're all top-tier scientists."

Flora's eyes sparkled with intrigue. "Did you know that 27% of them are Nobel laureates? An invitation from such a group is an honor!"

Ever the supportive spouse, Flora believed her husband to be the world's most remarkable man. Her belief in my abilities was unyielding, a trait I both admired and found amusing. I grasped her hand with a playful smile. "Darling, you misunderstand. To them, life is a series of equations and atomic structures. Interacting with them might just be the dullest endeavor."

Flora countered, "Yet, if they have reached out to you, they must face a challenge beyond their grasp–"

She paused, her eyes searching mine. "These are individuals who have made monumental contributions to humanity. Are you not compelled to aid them in their time of need?"

Her words, tinged with earnestness, made me chuckle. Flora's perspectives were often refreshingly unique.

"If we go together," I mused, "we'll treat it as a vacation."

Flora shook her head, teasingly. "I won't join you. Didn't you just say it's dull to mingle with such scientists?"

I stretched languidly. "Alright, but first, a call to Tanaka Maisaichi is in order. I must ascertain the nature of this conundrum before embarking on any journey."

With a hint of excitement, Flora agreed, "I'll connect the call for you."

As she dialed, my mind raced. What quandary could possibly necessitate my involvement within Vienna's scientific circles? I speculated wildly, yet each hypothesis seemed implausible. The phone interrupted my thoughts, and Flora handed me the receiver.

A woman's voice greeted me, "Professor Tanaka will join shortly. Please hold."

I glanced at the clock, its hands ticking steadily. Fortunately, the wait was brief. A familiar yet distant voice broke the silence, "Tanaka Maisaichi speaking. Who is this?"

Our previous encounters had been few, so I dispensed with formalities. "I received a telegram from your association. May I ask what requires my attention?"

His response was urgent, his breath quickening. "Mr. Morris, please, come to us. I am certain you can solve this dilemma!"

My patience thinned. "I must first understand the nature of this problem before I can even consider such a request."

The urgency in Tanaka Maisaichi's voice was palpable, his words tumbling out like a rushing stream. "It's delicate," he began, "we suspect it might be a murder. Yet, the police, after consulting us, insist it's a suicide. That's why I urged them to contact you!"

I couldn't help but chuckle, my voice rising in mock exasperation. "Mr. Tanaka, you've confused me with a private detective. I'm afraid that's a mistake."

"No, no!" Tanaka Maisaichi's voice was insistent. "Remember? You once mentioned your fascination with the inexplicable. Perhaps you'll reconsider once you learn who the deceased is."

Curiosity piqued, though still feigning disinterest, I asked, "Who?"

"Dr. Connors," he replied.

The name hit me like a lightning strike, rendering me momentarily speechless. Dr. Connors' death had been global news, his suicide a shocking revelation. A luminary in modern science, celebrated and mourned worldwide, Dr. Connors had left an indelible mark on the scientific community. At 52, his departure was sudden, the details of his death broadcasted widely—except perhaps in the remotest corners of the globe.

Reports confirmed his suicide, yet the Vienna Scientists Association harbored doubts of foul play. If indeed murdered, the implications could be vast, perhaps even embroiling political intrigue, given Connors' cutting-edge work. His latest breakthrough promised to revolutionize intercontinental travel, envisioning rockets that could render supersonic aircraft obsolete, shrinking America-Asia travel to a mere two hours.

A breath caught in my throat as I queried, "The reports claim suicide. What leads you to suspect otherwise?"

"We have... a film," Tanaka Maisaichi admitted. "Not conclusive evidence, but compelling enough for you to witness."

After a moment's deliberation, I acquiesced, "Very well, I'll come."

Tanaka Maisaichi's gratitude was effusive as I hung up, turning to find Flora's wide-eyed gaze fixed on me. I shrugged, bemused. "I never imagined I'd find myself entangled in the death of such a scientific titan!"

Flora had urged me to accept, but now the gravity of the situation, involving Dr. Connors' mysterious demise, weighed heavily on her. The potential for unspeakable danger loomed large.

Before she could voice her apprehensions, I preempted, "I've given my word, Darling. I can't retract it now."

She sighed, "Promise me one thing."

I nodded, and she continued, "If your initial investigation proves this is beyond personal resolution, promise you'll step away."

Her meaning was clear—if Connors' death was a casualty of political machinations, it was not my battle to fight. I agreed, "Rest assured, I believe the media reports. Connors took his own life. The notion of scientists playing detectives is rather amusing."

Flora smiled gently, "Don't underestimate their training. Scientists apply rigorous methodologies. If they doubt, there's a reason."

I chuckled, "Let's hope so."

As I boarded the flight bound for Vienna, my mind replayed every detail of Connors' death. The reports, exhaustive and seemingly irrefutable, pointed to suicide. Yet, the scientists' skepticism lingered, an enigma demanding resolution.

Upon arrival at Victoria Airport, I was greeted by Tanaka Maisaichi and three young scientists. Despite their youth, in Vienna, even those fresh-faced could have authored world-altering research.

Tanaka Maisaichi introduced me to the trio, each bearing the title of Doctor. The first, Dr. Lai Duan, was a striking blonde who looked more like a movie star than an atomic dynamics doctor. The second, Dr. Oga, was beginning to gain weight and showed signs of balding; he was a renowned figure in the study of epigraphy. The third, Dr. Anqiaojia, was tall and thin with a distinctively gypsy appearance—a fitting look for a mechanics doctor, whose name later turned out to be a true reflection of his heritage.

As we exited the terminal, I voiced my findings, "I've scrutinized Dr. Connors' death reports. Everything indicates suicide."

Dr. Lai Duan, exuding movie-star charisma, replied with a smile, "Visit his residence, and you'll be even more convinced of suicide."

Perplexed, I asked, "Then why summon me if suicide is certain?"

Anqiaojia explained, "We lack evidence but harbor suspicions, hence your involvement."

Dr. Tanaka interjected, "We intend to compensate you as a first-class detective."

I laughed, "If this piques my interest, payment won't be necessary."

Dr. Oga inquired eagerly, "When can you start?"

"Immediately," I assured them, ready to unravel the mystery of Dr. Connors' death.

As we stepped out of the airport and into the parking lot, Anqiaojia added, "If you're ready to start immediately, we'll take you to Dr. Connors's residence first."

Oga chimed in, "We'll show you the basis for our suspicions. After that, you'll be on your own; we're too busy to accompany you further."

I chuckled, "If it turns out to be a complex and twisted murder case, your company would be of little help anyway."

The four of them laughed, and Tanaka excused himself. Soon, he returned driving a large RV.

Scientists, though often seen as uninteresting, possess an admirable trait—their dedication to the idea that science transcends borders. True scientists regard knowledge as a gift to humanity, free from nationalistic confines. In our vehicle, we embodied this spirit: a Japanese, a Gypsy, a Scandinavian, an Irish American, and myself—a mix as diverse as the science we revered.

Tanaka drove us to the suburbs, and within half an hour, Dr. Connors' house emerged from the landscape. I recognized it from photographs—a modest structure, half-hidden among trees, crafted from romantic red pine wood.

As we approached on a gravel road, the scent of red pine filled the air. Two men blocked our path. Anqiaojia whispered, "National Security Agency."

I wasn't surprised. For someone like Connors, government interest was expected.

The agents peered inside, recognizing the scientists but scrutinizing me. One asked, "And who is this?"

Oga answered, "Mr. Ash Morris, invited for the investigation."

The agents frowned, skeptical. "What's there to investigate?"

Oga replied, "Even if Dr. Connors committed suicide, we want to understand why."

Reluctantly, the agents waved us through, and we parked before the house.

The residence was well-maintained. As we exited the vehicle, another guard, alerted by radio, opened the door for us.

Inside, we found ourselves in a spacious reception room—or rather, a massive study. Bookshelves lined all four walls, overflowing with volumes. Books covered the floor, chairs, and every conceivable surface, a testament to Connors' intellectual appetite.

Tanaka gestured at the chaos, "Nothing's been moved since Dr. Connors passed."

I surveyed the room, unable to resist commenting, "He must have been a bibliophile—and perhaps a solitary soul."

Oga nodded, "Indeed, he lived alone."

Anqiaojia added, "He wouldn't even let his housekeeper tidy these books!"

I smiled, "Some people thrive in chaos, shunning order."

We navigated through the room, the silent guard trailing behind. We reached an oak door. Tanaka tried the handle, but it was locked. The guard stepped forward, unlocking it. Beyond lay a study, or perhaps a studio, its centerpiece a massive desk piled high with books. Thick curtains muted the room's light, casting it in shadow.

As I turned to speak with Tanaka, I noticed a heavy bolt on the oak door, its opposite end pried open, the door frame splintered. This scene was familiar; Dr. Connors' body had been found after the door was forced open. It had been bolted from the inside at the time of his death.

We entered the room, Oga gesturing dramatically, "Mr. Morris, you're familiar with this place. Here, the century's greatest scientific mind met his end–"

He indicated the plush chair behind the desk.

I nodded, "Yes, he died from a poison injection, heart paralysis. It was a painless death."

Tanaka Maisaichi sighed, "Yes, with the door bolted shut and the windows double-layered for soundproofing, he was completely alone. Every window was secured."

I glanced at the scientists, "If you suspect murder, this is the classic 'locked room mystery.'"

The scientists appeared contemplative, while the guard shrugged, barely concealing his impatience. His expression suggested that, were it not for manners, he'd have laughed at the notion of a mysterious murder.

Ignoring the security guard's skepticism, I pointed to the carpet beside the chair. "The syringe that delivered the fatal dose was found here, bearing only Dr. Connors' fingerprints."

I paused, letting the gravity of the detail sink in. "Additionally, the pharmacist confirmed that Dr. Connors himself purchased the poison the day before his death."

The three scientists—Oga, Anqiaojia, and Tanaka Maisaichi—nodded in agreement. They had to; my remarks were drawn from an exhaustive report, meticulously detailing the circumstances of Connors' demise.

The room was silent, each breath audible as we absorbed the implications. I crossed to the window, pulling back the heavy drapes to flood the room with light. Methodically, I checked each window, though I knew it was futile. No one could have bolted the windows from inside and then exited.

Standing by the window, I surveyed the landscape of grass and trees, then turned to face them. "From where I'm standing, the National Security Agency's conclusion holds. Dr. Connors' death was a suicide, a conclusion that seems beyond dispute."

Oga, Anqiaojia, and Tanaka exchanged glances, a silent conversation passing among them.

"What puzzles me," I continued, "is why you still harbor doubts. What evidence prompts your suspicion?"

Anqiaojia's voice rose with conviction. "We do have evidence. We've obtained a substantial collection of film—"

Tanaka intervened smoothly, "Perhaps, An, it would be best to start from the beginning."

Oga gestured to the chairs, "Let's sit. There's no need to stand."

I obliged, my curiosity piqued. Connors' suicide seemed irrefutable from all angles. What had they uncovered to challenge such certainty?

As we settled into our seats, the anticipation was palpable. Anqiaojia, eager to share their findings, began to recount the story behind the film.

Chapter 2

Tracking and Filming Videos

As we settled into our seats, Anqiaojia began his story. "Let's start with Henry. He's a fourteen-year-old messenger boy."

I raised an eyebrow but let him continue.

Anqiaojia glanced at me, gauging my reaction. "Henry's a diligent kid, quite the positive spirit. Three days after Dr. Connors' death, he came to me with a large parcel wrapped in brown paper."

Despite the narrative's detours, I held my tongue, intrigued.

Anqiaojia continued his tale with a hint of amusement. "Henry was practically bursting with excitement. He said, 'Professor, guess what I've stumbled upon?' I advised him to turn it over to the police, but he was insistent. He'd found a package filled with tiny film reels, unlike any ordinary movies. His smile was secretive, almost mischievous."

He paused, gauging my reaction before continuing. "You know how perceptive kids can be these days. I could tell he was hinting at something significant. I playfully ruffled his hair, suggesting he avoid getting me involved. Yet, Henry persisted, wanting me to keep the package. Pressed for time, I agreed, thinking I'd later explain how to handle it properly. So, I let him leave it at my place."

Anqiaojia took a moment, collecting his thoughts, while I waited patiently, knowing he was building up to something crucial.

"Henry didn't return for a couple of days, perhaps he'd forgotten," Anqiaojia resumed. "Then, one evening, Tanaka and Oga dropped by for a chat."

He gestured to his colleagues. "During our conversation, I mentioned Henry's package. Oga suggested we take a look, as we had nothing better to do. Upon inspection, we discovered the films were ultra-small, much smaller than the usual 8mm. They required a specialized projector. Such films are rarely used, typically reserved for scientific purposes."

Tanaka chimed in, "Botanists, for instance, use this kind of film to document plant growth. By capturing one frame per minute, they can condense a month of growth into a few minutes of footage."

He looked at me to ensure I followed. I nodded, understanding the context, appreciating the meticulous nature of scientific documentation.

"The films piqued our curiosity," Anqiaojia continued. "If they were used as Dr. Tanaka described, they could potentially document activities over an extended period—possibly years. I didn't have the necessary projector, but the Scientist Association did. So, we decided to take the films there."

Oga interjected, "An, let's not dwell too long on how we found the films. Mr. Morris should see them for himself."

I asked, "If these films suggest another cause for Dr. Connors' death, why aren't they with the National Security Agency?"

Oga explained, "We did hand them over, but they returned them, stating they couldn't substantiate an alternative cause of death."

I refrained from probing further, knowing I'd soon see the footage. We rose, escorted by the security guard, and headed to the Scientist Association. Silence accompanied us until we reached the door. Oga asked, "We've invited interested members. Do you mind them joining us?"

"Not at all," I replied, intrigued by what lay ahead.

Tanaka added, "They're eager for your insights. The films run six hours and eleven minutes. I hope you won't be bored."

I was taken aback, having never committed to such a lengthy viewing. Yet, considering the subject matter—Dr. Connors—the prospect was fascinating.

Inside a spacious room, over thirty people awaited. Scientists prioritize efficiency, so Tanaka didn't introduce each person individually. Instead, he introduced me briefly and then proceeded to open a large wooden box of neatly arranged film reels. "Each reel covers ten days."

I nodded, eager to begin. "Please, let's start."

Tanaka summoned a staff member to set up a projector and screen. As the lights dimmed, silence fell. The projector whirred, and I pulled up a chair.

The first images were of pedestrians, their movements sped up by the time-lapse effect. Superimposed subtitles revealed the date: February 2-12, 1970.

Then, Dr. Connors appeared on screen. I recognized him instantly, having seen his photos countless times. The room watched in rapt attention as the films began to reveal their secrets.

As the films continued, I observed Dr. Connors amidst the bustling pedestrians, briefcase in hand, moving with purpose. The camera consistently followed him, capturing his routine: entering buildings, exiting, commuting, teaching, returning home, and repeating the cycle. Despite the fast-paced, almost comedic sequence of his movements due to the time-lapse, the monotony was evident.

With each reel, spanning ten-day increments, the narrative remained largely unchanged. Connors was consistently depicted in his daily activities, from professional engagements to mundane errands. By the fifteenth reel, I felt a surge of impatience. "Are the subsequent films all the same?" I asked.

Tanaka Maisaichi confirmed, "More or less. The variations are minor. Connors visited different locations occasionally, like a brief fishing trip during his semi-annual leave. But it's all documented."

I stood up, exasperated. "Okay, there's no need to continue."

The projection halted, lights flickered on, and the audience rose. A young man approached, questioning, ""Have you come to a conclusion after only watching a little and a half?"

Momentarily taken aback, I replied, "If they're all repetitive, why continue?"

The young man looked at me, wanting to say something but a bit speechless.

I smiled at him and said, "Young man, just say what's on your mind."

He hesitated, then spoke, "Pardon my directness, but your approach seems unscientific. You're inferring the whole from just part of it, correct?"

His words struck me, a reminder of the meticulous nature of scientific inquiry. I felt a twinge of embarrassment, acknowledging the rigor required to achieve scientific excellence—a rigor I momentarily bypassed.

As I pondered, Tanaka Maisaichi seemed ready to intercede and smooth things over. However, I preemptively agreed, "This gentleman is right. Let's continue watching."

Tanaka signaled the projector operator, and the "rustling" resumed.

We viewed the remaining reels, a commitment of six hours and eleven minutes. During intermissions, we ate sandwiches, sustaining our focus.

The latter half mirrored the initial reels, chronicling Connors' outdoor activities. The final reel, dated February 1, 1972, marked exactly one year of footage.

Throughout the year, every outdoor movement of Dr. Connors was meticulously captured at one frame per minute. The exhaustive documentation was both impressive and overwhelming, reinforcing the thoroughness of the surveillance.

As the screening concluded, I contemplated the implications. The films captured every nuance of Connors' public life, yet offered no obvious clues beyond his routine. The question remained: what was the significance of this exhaustive surveillance?

As the lights came back on, I could feel the weight of the room's anticipation. The group had grown, with more people joining midway through the screening, eager to hear my insights.

I addressed them directly. "Ladies and gentlemen, the films clearly show that for an entire year, someone meticulously monitored Dr. Connors' every outdoor movement, documenting it with extraordinary patience and resources."

Nods of agreement rippled through the audience.

I continued, "This kind of surveillance isn't undertaken lightly. It requires significant human and financial investment, suggesting a purposeful intent."

The crowd remained attentive, nodding in concurrence.

Taking a deep breath, I ventured further, "I understand why there's suspicion surrounding Dr. Connors' death. The logic follows that if someone tracked him so diligently for a year, it could have been with the intent to harm him."

A murmur spread through the room, but it soon quieted down.

Tanaka spoke up, affirming, "Exactly, that's our line of thinking."

I pressed on, "However, there's a crucial detail that might have been overlooked. The films only capture Dr. Connors' activities outside his home. There's no footage of his time indoors. If these recordings were meant to facilitate an assassination, it would be unlikely for Dr. Connors to die inside his own house."

Anqiaojia offered a wry smile, acknowledging, "That's also what the Security Bureau pointed out."

The room fell into a contemplative silence. While the surveillance was exhaustive, the lack of indoor footage posed a significant gap in the theory of an orchestrated murder. If the intent were truly to assassinate, the act wouldn't logically occur in the one place that wasn't recorded.

The mystery deepened, leaving us to ponder the true purpose behind such intense surveillance. While the films raised suspicions, they simultaneously cast doubt, leaving the circumstances of Dr. Connors' death shrouded in ambiguity.

I continued, "Furthermore, it's unnecessary to have a year-long record. In just the first ten days, there were countless opportunities to harm Dr. Connors in myriad ways."

The room was silent, the weight of my words hanging heavily in the air.

I shrugged, "These films only prove Dr. Connors was under close surveillance for a year. They don't confirm he was murdered."

A murmur of private conversations rippled through the room. Oga then spoke up, "The idea of someone tracking Dr. Connors so closely is unsettling. While our contributions to science may not rival his, none of us want to be subjected to such detailed surveillance."

I realized the deeper reason for my invitation. The scientific community was concerned about privacy and the implications of such invasive monitoring.

To be candid, all evidence points to Dr. Connors' death being a suicide. Yet, the films introduce new questions: who created them, and why?

I turned to Anqiaojia, "I can look into this, but I assume the security department has already done so. For someone as renowned as Dr. Connors to be tracked this way is indeed extraordinary."

Anqiaojia nodded, "True, but the security bureau hasn't found anything."

I pressed, " You haven't told me where Henry found this bag of films?"

Anqiaojia replied, "It's not that I haven't told you—I simply don't know. Henry hasn't revealed the location."

I hesitated, "What do you mean? He refuses to tell?"

Anqiaojia smiled bitterly and said, "No, since that day he gave me the package of films, I haven't seen him again. He disappeared!"

I was stunned again. A teenager had vanished. This clearly had the undertones of a crime.

The matter had taken a new turn. There was now another clue to pursue—starting with investigating Henry's disappearance. His vanishing was undoubtedly linked to this mysterious matter.

I asked, "Didn't the security bureau find him?"

Anqiaojia shook his head. "They searched, but there were no results."

I furrowed my brows, pondering the security bureau's lack of progress. Could I uncover something they hadn't? Regardless, my curiosity was piqued, and I felt compelled to investigate. "Everyone, I promise to do my best, though I can't guarantee results."

A few chuckled, acknowledging the shared challenge. "That's what each of us did," someone remarked.

Feeling the day's weight, I yawned. "I'm sorry, I need to rest now. Goodbye, everyone."

Tanaka, Anqiaojia, and Oga escorted me to the hotel. Once settled, I called Flora, summarizing the day's events in a lengthy conversation. Showered and ready for bed, I found sleep elusive.

The evidence was clear: Dr. Connors' death was a suicide. The poison, purchased by Connors himself, bore only his fingerprints.

Furthermore, Connors died in his studio. At the time, all the doors and windows were securely fastened from the inside. It was impossible for anyone to leave after committing the crime while keeping the doors and windows in this locked state.

His body was discovered in a locked room, seemingly eliminating the possibility of foul play. Yet, the six hours spent watching the films lingered in my mind.

These films documented a year's worth of Connors' outdoor activities, captured by an unknown observer. The intent behind this surveillance was a mystery.

If this person intended to kill Dr. Connors, they had multiple opportunities. A long-range rifle with a silencer could have done the job, and such weapons are readily available in this country. Had Dr. Connors been murdered now, the culprit might never be suspected. Yet, From the evidence, it appeared Dr. Connors committed suicide beyond a doubt.

I was perplexed. After mulling it over, I concluded that finding the person who had been shadowing Dr. Connors was crucial. This individual held the key to further progress.

To locate this person, I needed to find Henry, the messenger who discovered the films. His disappearance might unlock the entire mystery. Determined, I decided to start by searching for Henry.

With the decision to find Henry made, I managed to catch a few hours of restless sleep. Waking before dawn, I knew I had to start early, given Henry's occupation as a newspaper boy.

As I left the hotel, the city was just beginning to stir. The streets were mostly empty, save for the occasional figure of a drunkard slumped on the sidewalk or in their cars—an odd contrast to the academic prestige of the city. It was a curious sight, these well-dressed individuals choosing the street over their homes, a mystery in itself.

I wandered through the quiet streets until I spotted the first newspaper boy on his bicycle. I waved him down, but he only slowed momentarily, calling out, "Sir, what's up?"

"I'm looking for someone named Henry," I replied.

The boy shook his head and continued, "Sorry, I can't help you. I'm busy!"

Undeterred, I pressed on. Soon, another young newspaper boy appeared. Learning from my earlier encounter, I flashed a ten-dollar note and called out, "Hey, young man, answer three questions, and this is yours!"

He stopped, eyeing me curiously. "You're not drunk?"

"No," I assured him. "I'm trying to find a newspaper boy named Henry."

"Henry? Yeah, I know him," the boy said, nodding. "The kid with freckles, right?"

Relieved, I confirmed, "That's him. Do you know where he is?"

"Haven't seen him in weeks," the boy replied. "What's your third question?"

Caught off guard by his efficiency, I quickly asked, "Do you know where he lives?"

He grinned, "Sure, 27A George Street. It's a small side street. From the city park, it's the sixth side street. He lives with his sister."

With that, he snatched the bill from my hand, whistled, and pedaled away.

I stood there, watching the scene unfold as the city came to life under the morning sun. Policemen began rousing the drunks.

One officer, with a practiced hand, helped a middle-aged man to his feet, nudging him awake from his drunken stupor. Groggy, the man eventually found his balance and stumbled off, leaving the sidewalk to the early risers and the city's routine bustle.

The officer spun around, fixing me with a gaze that seemed to pierce the morning fog. "Can you believe it?" he asked, his voice laced with irony. "That drunkard over there, when sober, could engage Einstein in a debate."

Intrigued, I leaned in. "A scientist, you say?"

He nodded, gesturing to the figure slumped in the car. "Every last one of them. The gentleman you just saw is a university professor."

As we approached a sleek, expensive car, I noticed a man inside, head lolled to the side, a faint trace of foam at his lips. The policeman rapped sharply on the roof. "Another professor," he remarked dryly. "I get to play alarm clock for about seventeen or eighteen of these geniuses every morning."

Curiosity piqued, I asked, "Why the drinking?"

The policeman's eyes widened in disbelief, as if I'd missed something obvious. "What else could they do? Their brains are wired to equations and theories. Time is a luxury they can't afford to waste, yet they live for the relentless advancement of science. For some, drunkenness is the only escape from their ceaseless grind."

The man in the car stirred, blinking at the policeman through foggy eyes. A sheepish grin spread across his face. "What time is it?"

The policeman supplied the hour, and the man jolted upright. "Damn, I'm late!" He slammed the accelerator, the car roaring to life and speeding away, leaving a trail of dust and urgency.

After getting detailed directions to George Street from the policeman, I decided to walk. The city was awakening, its pulse quickening with the influx of pedestrians and the hum of traffic. There was a frenetic energy, a race against time as everyone hurried toward their destinations.

The sight of so many intellectuals sprawled in the streets before dawn was a jarring contrast to the vibrant life now unfolding. I navigated through the park, along wide sidewalks, past historical buildings that bore witness to decades gone by, until I reached the storied George Street.

The architecture spoke of a bygone era, buildings standing as silent sentinels, whispering tales of their 70 or 80-year tenure. Children skipped past, their laughter a bright counterpoint to the solemnity of the street.

I arrived at number 27A, just as a housewife emerged, collecting bottles of milk from the doorstep. I seized the opportunity, bounding up the steps. "Good morning. I'm looking for Henry."

She gave me a cursory glance, pushed the door open, and pointed silently down a stairway before disappearing upstairs.

Descending the stairs, I found myself before a door. I knocked, the sound echoing in the narrow hallway. No answer. I knocked again, harder this time.

A gruff voice finally barked from within, "Who are you looking for?"

Taken aback, I hesitated. The voice was unexpected, masculine. The boy had mentioned only Henry and his sister. Had I been misled?

The door swung open to reveal a man who seemed more beast than human, his frame broad and imposing. Shirtless, he filled the doorway, eyes narrowing as they fixed on me. "Excuse me," I stammered, "is Henry here?"

The man's stare was unreadable, a puzzle wrapped in muscle and mystery, leaving me to wonder if I had just stumbled upon another piece of the intricate puzzle surrounding Henry's disappearance.

CHAPTER 3

BEHIND CUTTING-EDGE SCIENCE

The man spat into the corridor with a dismissive "Puh," the saliva narrowly missing me and intensifying the discomfort of our interaction.

"Henry? Haven't seen him in two weeks," he grumbled, his voice gravelly. "Don't bother me with this."

"Excuse me," I ventured, trying to gauge his connection to Henry, "who are you to Henry?"

The question seemed to amuse him. He let out a rough laugh. "I'm not nobody to him!"

Sensing an opportunity, I pressed further. "Then, can I see his room?"

The man's laughter echoed louder, mocking my request. "His room? Sure, go ahead, take a look!"

He stepped back, allowing me to enter.

Inside, I was immediately taken aback. Despite having only arrived yesterday, I knew this city was renowned for its universities and scientific institutions, symbolizing the pinnacle of modern human civilization.Until now, all I had seen were magnificent buildings and neat, elegant small houses. I couldn't comprehend why there were so many drunks on the streets, and now I was equally baffled by the existence of such shallow, narrow, and dark residential units in this city.

The so-called living room was a jumble of worn-out furniture, leading to a kitchen and a closed door that presumably led to a bedroom. Suppressing my surprise, I kept my expression neutral, aware of the man's volatile demeanor.

"Henry's room is—" I began, but he interrupted, kicking a chair aside and swinging open a closet door. "Here!"

The truth hit me hard. Henry didn't have a room. His "room" was a tiny closet, scarcely large enough for a child. No wonder the man had laughed.

The closet was a chaotic mix of youthful belongings—picture books, a baseball glove, scattered books—yet nothing of immediate significance.

As I rummaged, a woman's voice drifted from the bedroom. "Johnny, who are you talking to?"

"A German!" the man called back.

I turned, correcting him. "I'm not German!"

Unfazed, he relayed my correction, then shrugged. "Does it matter? So long as you're human, it's fine, right?"

His unexpected insight caught me off guard. For a man seemingly rough around the edges, his words hinted at a deeper understanding.

A woman emerged, her hair disheveled, cigarette in hand. She exhaled a plume of smoke, surveying me with a mix of curiosity and amusement. "Looking for Henry again? He's been gone a while. You're too late."

Stunned, I asked, "Are you Henry's sister?"

She nodded, taking another drag from her cigarette, her demeanor nonchalant.

"Forgive me," I pressed, "if Henry's missing, why not report it to the police?"

She chuckled, a sound devoid of worry. "A young man leaving this place? It's not surprising. It's dreadful here, isn't it?"

"If it's so terrible," I countered, "why not try to improve it?"

Her laughter was sharp and knowing. "Oh, we've improved. We came from somewhere worse. We're satisfied now. Why change?"

I was taken aback. "Is there truly somewhere worse in your country?"

The pair laughed, their shared history evident. The man spoke, "Many places are worse. But most lack the courage to escape like we did."

Their words painted a picture of escapees, fugitives from the very heart of academia. I stood there, absorbing this unexpected revelation.

The woman took another drag, her voice tinged with disdain. "The university forum, the bleak library, the lifeless research institute, the endless science—it's all dreadful. We've escaped that nightmare. I'm no longer Dr. Padella, and he's not Professor Han Jingni. What do you think of us now?"

I was truly stunned. Her words rang with a truth I couldn't dismiss. Could this really be the world they fled from—one of intellectual imprisonment?

The reality of their escape, from the very institutions revered by society, challenged my understanding. It seemed that beneath the veneer of progress and prestige lay a hidden world of personal rebellion and liberation.

At that moment, words failed me. I simply shook my head, the weight of the encounter pressing down on me. The woman sauntered over, draping her arms around the broad shoulders of the man beside her. I stammered, "So, what are you doing now?"

With a nonchalant gesture, she pointed at the man's rugged features. "He delivers goods for a laundry shop, and I clean floors. We're content, much happier than those too afraid to break free. But Henry... he doesn't see it that way. He wants out. We all choose our paths. I can't force him back, can I?"

A strange unease settled over me as I listened. The two of them seemed a touch unconventional, their choices baffling yet oddly intriguing.

Reluctantly, I took my leave, murmuring apologies as I backed towards the door. I had extracted nothing of value from this encounter. Just as I reached the threshold, the woman seemed to recall something, her finger darting towards me. "Oh, by the way, Henry showed me something before he vanished. Said he found it. Want to take a look?"

Curiosity piqued despite myself, I nodded. "Okay."

She crossed the room to a table, rummaging through a drawer until she unearthed a piece of cardboard. The chaos of clutter parted, revealing the artifact she'd mentioned.

The cardboard was roughly a foot square, and as she handed it to me, I studied it closely. It was a bewildering array of straight lines, some repeated so frequently they formed thickened paths, others more sparsely drawn. Among them, a pentagonal shape emerged, alongside triangles and quadrilaterals of varying sizes.

"What is this?" I asked, perplexed.

She shrugged. "No idea. If you want it, take it. Doesn't matter to me."

Though seemingly useless, the cardboard's origin intrigued me. It was found by Henry, after all, and who knew what secrets those lines might hold? I tucked it under my arm. "Thank you."

As I stepped outside, the man and woman faded into the backdrop of the city, leaving me to breathe deeply of the fresh air. The morning had been spent chasing shadows, seeking any trace of Henry. Even the police had nothing to offer; no missing person report had been filed.

By noon, I found myself back at the hotel. After a quick lunch, I made my way to the Scientists Association, a place where I was granted free rein, thanks to Tanaka Maisaichi's instructions.

Upon arrival, I sank into a plush sofa, a steaming cup of coffee swiftly provided by the attentive staff. As I sipped, Anqiaojia joined me. Despite his status as an authoritative scientist, his gait still retained the distinctive swagger of a gypsy.

"Any progress?" he inquired, settling across from me.

"Not really," I admitted, recounting my encounter with Henry's sister.

Anqiaojia's brow furrowed. "And what good does that do you?"

I leaned forward, a name on my lips. "Have you ever heard of a researcher named Padella?"

He chuckled. "This city is teeming with researchers. Hard to keep track of them all."

"But this Padella is different," I insisted. "She described her lab as a hellish place, fled, and now works as a cleaner."

To my surprise, Anqiaojia remained unfazed. "This isn't unusual. There are many people like that. I know of a scientist whom several universities are vying to hire, but instead, he chooses to work as a gardener in the park."

I was taken aback. "Really? Why?"

He paused, a contemplative look in his eyes. "Psychiatrists call it occupational fatigue, but I think it's the crushing pressure."

I looked at Anqiaojia with a somewhat puzzled expression. His demeanor was very serious. "Human life is limited. To become a scientist, you must spend at least one-third of your life in study. The other two-thirds are spent in nearly the same situation, save for slight differences in material life. This pressure compels many to abandon everything they've achieved and return to ordinary lives. In short, the life of a scientist is consuming. Some prefer to relinquish it all for a simpler existence."

I shrugged, attempting levity. "I can't get it. Would you ever walk away from your research to join a caravan."

His expression turned grave, and I immediately I regretted my jest. But, Anqiaojia, despite his roots, was a man of vast knowledge, not easily offended.

After a moment's silence, he spoke, his voice laden with nostalgia. "Last year, I went to Europe and met the tribe I was born into, near the Hungarian border. My great uncle was still there and asked me, 'Child, what are you doing?' I told him, 'I am now a scientist!' He asked again, 'Child, what do scientists do?' I explained in the simplest words, 'We study science to make human life better!'

Anqiaojia paused for a moment, glancing at me. "He still didn't understand, so I roughly explained my daily work. Guess what he said after hearing it."

I retorted, "What did he say?"

Anqiaojia's smile was tinged with bitterness as he recalled his great-uncle's words. "His voice trembled when he said, 'Poor child, your life seems so dull now. You should come back. We may not have science, but we have singing, dancing, and endless joy.'"

He paused, letting the weight of his words settle. "So, if you think I don't long to return to my gypsy roots and that carefree life, you're mistaken."

I swallowed hard, the implications of his confession sinking in. Anqiaojia stretched, his demeanor shifting. "Dr. Connors, you see, wasn't the first to take his own life. But those videos... they demand our investigation."

I sighed, glancing out onto the streets. "No wonder I see so many well-dressed drunks out there."

Anqiaojia chuckled, a mischievous glint in his eye. "That's nothing unusual. I've been drunk on the streets myself, even gotten into a few scuffles. It's quite the thrill!"

I waved my hand dismissively, trying to steer the conversation back. "Henry disappeared after meeting you and handing over that film. He also had this card paper." I unrolled it, revealing the cryptic lines. "What do you make of this?"

Anqiaojia scrutinized the paper, examining it from every angle before shaking his head. "I can't say. It resembles some kind of crystal structure, like something you'd see under a microscope."

"Does it have any scientific value?" I probed.

He frowned thoughtfully. "Hard to tell. But when more of our colleagues gather this evening, we might find an answer."

"Okay, let's leave it here for now," I said, deciding not to carry the piece of paper around as I doubted its usefulness.

During the day, not many people visited, and Anqiaojia left soon after.

I spent the entire afternoon searching for Henry's whereabouts throughout the city. I broadened my network of contacts, but the result remained the same. No one had seen Henry in the past two weeks.

I had no choice. Henry might have left the city or encountered an unpredictable accident, but I couldn't find any clues.

I turned to Dr. Connors' acquaintances to investigate his life.

My investigation spanned several days but went smoothly. The people who knew Dr. Connors were part of the scientific community, and since they had invited me, they answered my questions as best they could.

Despite the smooth progress, my gains were minimal. Over the past few days, I learned that Dr. Connors was obsessed with science. He lived a simple life with a good income, most of which was invested in real estate managed by a reputable company.

This company was beyond doubt. They had sorted out Dr. Connors' estate and donated it to the university authorities.

No one could benefit from Connors' death; people only felt loss. If this was the case, who would kill him? His death was a suicide, without a doubt.

Everyone I spoke to echoed the same sentiment: Connors' death was a suicide. Yet mysteries lingered—Henry's disappearance, the enigmatic man seen with Connors two days before his death, and the perplexing film footage.

I had spoken with Connors' housekeeper several times. According to them, the doctor was typically silent at home, only speaking when visitors came. I spent most of my day investigating the doctor's visitors, identifying each one except for one.

This anomaly seemed significant enough to record in detail.

According to the housekeeper, a "thin, about fifty years old, brown-haired, half bald, with eyes as sharp as a hawk" man visited the doctor two days before his death. This stranger spoke with the doctor for a while before they both left together, returning about two hours later.

There was nothing extraordinary about this encounter, except that I couldn't identify this man. He clearly wasn't part of the doctor's usual circle. After this visit, the man disappeared, never to be seen again.

I had two artists sketch the person based on the housekeeper's description. Once the housekeeper was satisfied with the likeness, I took the drawing to the police.

In the police officer's office, I met with setback. The officer informed me that there were at least 3,000 men in the city who matched the description in the sketch!

I resumed my search for the man but found nothing. It seemed there was no turning point, and staying any longer felt meaningless.

In my experience, few cases are as inconclusive as this one. Yet, there was nothing more I could do.

I had been commissioned to investigate Dr. Connors' death, and in that regard, I had a conclusion: Connors committed suicide, beyond any doubt.

However, doubts remained. Without reasonable explanations for the film recording Dr. Connors' outdoor activities for a year, Henry's disappearance, and the identity of the mysterious man, the case remained open-ended.

As I prepared to leave, I felt a deep sense of dissatisfaction. The Scientist Association held a farewell party for me the night before. Aware of my lack of breakthroughs, no one mentioned Dr. Connors.

The next morning, I didn't want anyone to see me off. I carried my suitcase, boarded the streetcar, and headed straight to the airport.

I arrived early, so after checking in my luggage, I sat down in the airport restaurant.

The overcast sky mirrored my mood. I replayed the events in my mind, searching for overlooked clues.

Amidst my reverie, I sensed a gaze upon me, an inexplicable intuition. I glanced up to find a young man observing me from a nearby table. Our eyes met, and rather than look away, he rose and approached.

With a confident smile, he asked, "Mind if I join you?"

Given my foul mood, my response came out more curtly than intended. "That depends on your purpose," I replied stiffly.

The young man maintained his composure, offering a polite smile. "I just want to talk to you, Mr. Morris. My name is Beck Bice, and here's my ID."

As he handed me his identification, I scrutinized it closely. The hostility I initially felt towards him began to ebb.

According to the ID, Beck Bice was a "special investigator" with the National Security Bureau.

I returned his smile. "Your name is quite intriguing. Please, have a seat."

Beck pulled out a chair and settled in, clasping his hands behind his head. For a brief moment, he seemed uncertain of how to proceed. "If you have something to say, say it quickly. I'm about to leave," I prompted.

Beck rubbed his hands together, choosing his words carefully. "Mr. Morris, I ask you not to leave. This isn't an official request; it's purely personal."

Despite his roundabout explanation, I appreciated Beck's clarity. It suggested he was both intelligent and methodical. I raised an eyebrow. "Why?"

"To put it bluntly, it's concerning Dr. Connors' death," Beck replied.

I frowned, ready to interject, but Beck hurriedly continued, "We've been aware of your presence since you arrived and have followed your investigation closely."

I chuckled. "So, why does the Bureau have an interest in me? I thought they were dismissive of this matter."

Beck laughed as well, gesturing with his hands. "The Bureau isn't ignoring it; they've entrusted it to me."

He paused, as if weighing his next words, "By assigning me this case, they're acknowledging its closure in legal terms. However, several questions remain. My role is not constrained by time or the need for a definitive conclusion because, officially, the case is closed."

I nodded. "I see. So you're a special investigator."

Beck admitted, "I've retraced your steps, yet it led to no results."

"Given that you aren't required to produce outcomes, it seems further investigation is unnecessary," I observed.

Beck shook his head. "Officially, yes, but personally, this is a challenge I cannot ignore."

He paused, his expression grave. "We know someone followed Dr. Connors for a year, an endeavor requiring substantial resources. No one undertakes such an effort without reason. Even if Connors' death was a suicide, the individual who tracked him likely played a significant role. We need to identify them to prevent a similar tragedy from befalling another scientist."

Beck's conviction was palpable, each word delivered with unwavering seriousness.

I couldn't help but feel a pang of skepticism. While I acknowledged the mysterious surveillance raised questions, I wasn't as convinced of his conclusions. "Those recordings remain a significant mystery, but I'm not ready to draw the same conclusions you have."

For a moment, I remained silent, letting the tension hang in the air. Then, Beck continued, "I'm also trying to track down Henry's whereabouts and the mysterious visitor who met with Dr. Connors, but—"

I interjected, spreading my hands in resignation, "No results there either, right?" Beck's expression soured with a hint of frustration. "Yes. This responsibility falls to me, and I need to clear up these uncertainties. I believe you might be able to assist."

"I can't do much," I admitted, feeling the weight of the unsolved puzzle.

"Perhaps we've missed something crucial, which is why we're at a dead end," Beck suggested.

"It's not that we lack clues," I countered. "Finding Henry and identifying the mysterious man would undoubtedly push things forward. The issue is they're nowhere to be found."

Beck's eyes locked onto mine with a newfound intensity. "I have some additional information regarding Henry."

My surprise was evident. "What is it?"

Beck hesitated, as if weighing the gravity of his words. "It might not directly relate to Henry, but it's another unsolved case that could be connected. A charred body was discovered in an abandoned car. The victim was determined to be a 13-year-old male. Beyond these facts, there's little else."

The news left me momentarily speechless. "Where and when was this?"

"The location is 1,300 miles from here, a small town," Beck explained. "The body was found three days after Henry disappeared."

I shook my head, skepticism creeping in. "It's highly implausible for a teenager to travel 1,300 miles in three days."

"Unless he flew," Beck suggested.

I chuckled at the notion. "Sure, but if he had flown, there'd be a record. I've already combed through airline passenger lists."

Beck sighed heavily. "I did the same."

I exhaled slowly, sharing in his frustration. "I assume your findings match mine."

Beck nodded, his expression weary. "Indeed. Henry never boarded a plane."

"So, there's no point dwelling on it further," I concluded. "The body in that small town can't be Henry."

Beck shook his head, disagreeing with my conclusion. "Not entirely. We've only looked into public airlines. There are many private planes we couldn't track."

His words caught me off guard. It was a plausible angle I hadn't considered. But why would anyone take Henry 1,300 miles away on a private plane just to kill him?

The notion that Henry had been taken was logical. A teenager couldn't easily arrange such a journey on his own. I glanced at Beck, who seemed to read my thoughts. "I believe Henry's death is linked to that bag of films he found."

I frowned, skepticism surfacing. "How could that be? Henry picked up those films by chance. He might not have known their owner. And if someone wanted him dead, why not do it here?"

"If it were me," Beck explained, "I wouldn't act here either. If Henry died in this city, the Security Bureau would immediately suspect a connection to Dr. Connors' death and those films. The lack of evidence wouldn't stop a large-scale investigation, which would be risky for the murderer."

I took a deep breath, lighting a cigarette to calm my thoughts. "So, what do you want from me?"

"I learned about the charred body just two days ago," Beck said. "Without evidence linking it to Henry, it's still under my jurisdiction. I plan to investigate that town, and I want you to join me."

The airport loudspeaker announced the final boarding call, but my mind was elsewhere. If Henry was indeed murdered, it warranted a deeper look into Dr. Connors' demise.

Beck's unwavering gaze stayed fixed on me as I mulled over the decision. As I finished my cigarette, I stubbed it out decisively and stood. "Alright, I'll go with you."

With that, a new chapter of our investigation began, promising answers—or at least more questions—waiting 1,300 miles away.

CHAPTER 4

TRACKING THE

TEENAGER'S WHEREABOUTS

Beck's exuberance was palpable, his grip firm as he shook my hands with uncontainable joy. "I need to hurry with the refund process," I said, a smile playing on my lips. "My luggage is already on the plane!"

Beck's expression shifted to one of contrition. "I'm so sorry for the trouble," he apologized earnestly. I chuckled, reassuring him, "This is exactly what I wanted to do."

With a swift but courteous reception from the airline staff, I navigated the necessary procedures and managed a long-distance call to ensure my luggage would be stored. Beck had anticipated my decision, securing two tickets in advance. It was as if he knew I couldn't resist the call of adventure.

Two hours later, we disembarked, greeted by an awaiting car at the airport—a clear indication that Beck's foresight was as sharp as ever. He drove us directly to the enigmatic town.

"If we can uncover who killed Henry, everything will fall into place," I suggested, eyes on the horizon, where the sun dipped low, casting long shadows.

Beck, ever the skeptic, shook his head. "I'm not as optimistic. For now, I just need to confirm that the dead man is indeed Henry."

There was no point in arguing; we were aligned in our pursuit of truth. The identity of the deceased had to be established before we could unravel the mystery further.

Upon reaching the town, our first stop was the police station. The local facility lacked the amenities to preserve a body, so after a comprehensive forensic examination, the remains had been buried, but meticulous records were kept.

Inside the police station, a stack of haunting photographs awaited us. The first image—a charred body slumped in the backseat of a scorched car—was a jarring sight. The vehicle reduced to a blackened skeleton, the body curled in a fetal position. Without prior knowledge, one might mistake the remains for a piece of charred wood.

As we reviewed the grim photos, a police officer approached. "We've conducted an exhaustive search," he reported. "No local teenagers are missing, so the boy is definitely from outside."

Beck and I exchanged a knowing glance. "Did anyone see the stranger?" I inquired.

In a town of merely a thousand souls, outsiders stood out like proverbial sore thumbs. My question was neither abrupt nor misplaced.

The officer nodded. "Yes, an old man witnessed a man and a boy early in the morning. Both were strangers, and the man seemed to be hurrying the boy along."

Beck's excitement was palpable. "Where is this old man? We must speak with him immediately!"

But the officer shook his head, a somber expression on his face. "After the body was discovered, we questioned him. He was the caretaker at the lumberyard where the body was found."

Beck, impatient, pushed further. "Regardless of who he is, we need to talk to him."

The officer replied with a wry smile, "Unfortunately, no one can speak to him now."

Beck and I, caught off guard, responded in unison, "Is he dead?"

The officer spread his hands wide in a gesture of helplessness. In that moment, without uttering a word, Beck and I understood the gravity of the situation. The case had taken a sinister turn.

I pressed, "Was his death an accident?"

The officer shrugged, "You could call it that. Or natural causes. He was a known drug addict. The doctor attributed his death to an overdose."

Beck, thoughtful, remained silent. I probed further, "How soon after speaking with you did he die?"

The officer seemed taken aback. "You suspect foul play?"

I nodded, but he shook his head dismissively. "No one would bother to kill Old Mike."

"But the murderer would," I insisted. "Old Mike saw the man, could describe him!"

The officer laughed, albeit awkwardly. "Old Mike was a notorious drunk and drug addict. He even claimed to have seen unicorns in the mountains. No one believed his tales. If the killer knew this, he wouldn't have bothered silencing him."

Beck, his voice cold and steady, countered, "We believe him."

The officer hesitated, his expression uneasy. I followed up, "Did you record Old Mike's account or sketch the strangers based on his description?"

The officer shrugged again, a gesture of resignation. "This is a small town. I'm just the sheriff here. My biggest challenge is dealing with vagrants and checking for drugs."

Beck cut him off with a wave. "Enough. Take us to where the boy was found."

The officer relaxed, his tone lightening. "Sure thing. Is this boy someone important?"

Beck's eyes pierced the officer with an intensity that left no room for indifference. "In our country," he declared, his voice steady and unwavering, "every life matters. When someone dies, regardless of their status, we owe it to them to uncover the truth."

The officer shrugged once more, a gesture of resignation that seemed to epitomize the lackadaisical approach of small-town law enforcement. But Beck and I, driven by a relentless pursuit of justice, found such attitudes unacceptable.

The officer led the way, his jeep kicking up a cloud of dust as we followed in our car, leaving the town behind. The road turned remote, winding into the rugged embrace of the mountains. Soon, the landscape bore the scars of a recent fire—blackened bushes lining the roadside, the skeletal remains of a car at its heart.

We stepped out, the acrid scent of ash still lingering in the air. Beck and I walked side by side, his voice cutting through the silence as he assessed the scene. "This was deliberate," he stated, eyes scanning the charred wreckage. "The arsonist used at least ten gallons of gasoline."

Despite my lack of expertise, I found myself nodding in agreement. Beck, ever the investigator, approached the car, his small knife scraping away the soot to reveal a sequence of numbers on the engine block—a vital clue to the car's origins.

I quickly jotted the numbers down, my mind racing with possibilities. The local police had clearly overlooked this detail, their laxity a stark contrast to our urgency.

Beck circled the car, testing the door handle. "It's locked," he noted grimly. "Poor Henry. If he was inside, he might have been trapped."

I remained silent, my skepticism about the boy's identity lingering. Beck was convinced it was Henry, but I needed more proof.

"If the boy is Henry," I mused aloud, "then he likely arrived here by plane. The car might have been rented from the nearest town with an airport. That narrows our search."

Beck nodded, frustration simmering beneath his calm exterior. He kicked the car in frustration before turning away. The officer, sensing our dissatisfaction, asked, "Find anything?"

Beck, his patience worn thin, replied curtly, "Nothing."

The officer, unfazed, continued with his theory. "My report says the boy was a car thief. Stole the car, crashed, and it caught fire."

Beck's incredulity was evident. "And who reported the car stolen?"

The officer shrugged again, his eyes wide with insouciance. "Who knows? I told you, he's from elsewhere."

I joined Beck, patting his shoulder as we returned to our car. Back in town, we checked into a hotel, our minds already racing ahead. Beck made call after call, reaching out to contacts across the country. What would have taken months in the pre-digital age took mere hours—by nightfall, we had our answer.

The car was a 1965 model, passed through numerous hands before ending up with a used car dealer in Green River City, a mere 120 miles from our current location. Importantly, Green River City had an airport.

Fueled by excitement, we drove to Green River City, the car eating up the miles under Beck's skillful control. Dawn was just breaking as we arrived, the city still wrapped in the quiet of early morning.

Finding the used car dealer was easy. He was a burly, bald man with a booming voice. "Bad luck on my part," he lamented. "You never know if a used car's stolen. Which one are you after?"

Beck cut to the chase. "We're not here for stolen cars. About two weeks ago, you sold a 1965 model. The engine number is–" He recited the number, and the dealer flipped through his ledger.

"Yes, the cheapest one," the dealer confirmed. "Sold it for 200 Dollar, but it was ancient."

Beck and I exchanged a glance, the pieces of the puzzle aligning. "Who bought it?" we pressed.

The dealer tilted his head, recalling the transaction. "A man and a boy. Came in about this time. Asked for the cheapest running car."

I produced the photos–one of the man, the other of Henry. "Were these the ones?"

The dealer glanced at them, nodding. "Yes, that's them. The man paid cash, quick and easy."

My heart raced, triumph surging through me. We had found someone else who had seen the mysterious man.

Beck's voice crackled with energy. "Did you ask for a driver's license? Check your records."

The dealer hesitated, a sheepish look crossing his face. Beck's patience snapped. "You didn't, did you? That's illegal!"

The old car dealer's discomfort was palpable, his forced smile doing little to mask his unease. "Sir," he stammered, rubbing his hands together nervously, "you have to understand, in a small place like this, sometimes we... well, we just try to accommodate our customers' needs."

His attempt at placation fell flat, and I saw Beck's face flush with anger, his fists clenching tightly. It was clear that he was on the brink of losing control, his frustration boiling over.

Sensing the impending eruption, I stepped forward just as Beck's patience snapped. He swung a fist at the dealer's ample midsection, but I managed to intervene in time, pushing Beck aside so that his punch landed harmlessly against a car door instead.

The sound reverberated with a metallic clang, leaving a deep dent in the panel—a testament to Beck's strength and training in karate. The car dealer stood frozen, his face pale, the fat on his cheeks quivering with fear.

"Beck, hitting him won't solve anything!" I shouted, trying to rein in my partner's fury.

Beck's voice was a guttural growl. "This fat pig's disregard for the law has thrown all our efforts into chaos!"

His words struck a chord. We were desperate to track down two key figures—Henry and the elusive stranger. If Henry had perished, identifying the stranger became paramount. A proper registration could have led us straight to him.

Despite my own frustration, I sought to calm Beck, hoping to defuse the tension. "Even if he had a driver's license, it could have been fake."

Beck's breathing was heavy, his anger still simmering beneath the surface. I turned back to the dealer, probing further. "What happened after the sale? Did they say anything that might help us?"

The dealer, eager to appease, replied quickly, "They drove off together, heading south."

That direction matched the location where the boy's body was found, reinforcing the grim possibility that the victim was indeed Henry.

I stepped closer, my hand resting firmly on the dealer's shoulder. "Try to remember. Did the man mention their origin or how they arrived in Green River City?"

The dealer, eyes wide with trepidation, shook his head. "I didn't hear anything specific—just the boy asking about their destination, and the man saying, 'Soon.'"

Beck, having regained some composure, joined us. His voice was cold, but his anger had abated. "Ash, let's move on. This guy's got nothing for us. Let's head to the airport."

I lingered for a moment, scrutinizing the dealer, but his fear was genuine; he had nothing more to offer.

Beck's instincts were right. Our next logical step was the airport. With the timeframe we were working with, Henry's arrival in Green River City almost certainly involved a flight.

As we left, Beck channeled his remaining frustration into the drive, the car's engine roaring as we sped toward the airport, determined to uncover the truth.

By the time we reached the airport, night had fully descended, casting a cloak of darkness over the sparse landscape. The airport was little more than a flat expanse, suitable only for the small planes that occasionally touched down. A row of modest buildings stood nearby, their windows glowing with light, hinting at the presence of people inside.

Beck, intent on making an impression, barreled the car toward the building, honking the horn with no regard for subtlety. The vehicle lurched to a halt, its sudden stop shaking us violently. A man emerged from the building, beer can in hand, his expression mirroring his irritation.

Beck stepped out, unfazed by the man's anger. "Pull a stunt like that again," the man barked, "and you'll regret it!"

With a cold, unwavering gaze, Beck presented his ID. The man's bravado faltered, his tone shifting to one of compliance. "Oh, Security Bureau. What brings you here?"

"Who's in charge here?" Beck demanded.

"That would be me," the man replied, attempting to regain his composure. "What do you need?"

"Let's discuss this inside," Beck insisted, moving toward the door.

The man blocked his path, panic creeping into his eyes. "No, you can't go in. Whatever you need, ask here."

Beck's suspicion flared. "We need the aircraft landing records from the past two weeks."

The man hesitated but relented, gesturing toward the office. "You'll find them there."

Beck's voice hardened. "What are you hiding inside? Why can't we enter?"

The man's demeanor shifted, his anxiety palpable. Beck, sensing deceit, pushed past him. The man reacted swiftly, swinging the beer can at Beck's head. Instinctively, I stepped in, deflecting the can with a swift motion, then countered with a strike that sent the man reeling into the door with a resounding thud.

A woman's voice pierced the tension, her tone weary. "Don't fight, George. Let them in. I'm done with this secretive life."

The voice belonged to a striking red-haired woman who emerged from the building, her expression one of indifference. Her presence momentarily defused the situation, and Beck, recognizing her influence, dropped his raised hand.

I couldn't suppress a wry smile. This investigation had unfolded in ways I hadn't anticipated—a mosaic of eccentric characters and unexpected encounters. From drunken professors to negligent officers, from clandestine lovers to opportunistic dealers, the underbelly of this country had revealed itself in full.

Beck, ever diplomatic, offered an apologetic smile to George and the woman. "We're not here to pry into your personal matters," he assured them. "We're just passing through, investigating a plane that landed here."

George, still tense, nodded and ushered the woman back inside. "Wait here," he instructed, disappearing with her.

After a few tense minutes, George returned, now wearing a coat. "Follow me to my office."

We refrained from questioning the arrangement he'd made with the red-haired woman, focusing instead on our objective. He led us to another building, where he flicked on the lights and retrieved a stack of documents from a filing cabinet.

The records held the key to our next move, each page a potential lead in our relentless pursuit of the truth.

Beck and I dove into the stack of documents, our eyes scanning the records with practiced efficiency. We focused on the day the used car dealer made his sale. Our search quickly zeroed in on a single entry: a landing by a Mr. Empero, accompanied by three friends, who had departed the same night. Clearly, they were not our targets.

Undeterred, we flipped back a page to the prior day's entries. Two planes had landed—one carrying a sports college student, the other three women on vacation. None matched our quarry.

Beck turned to George, his expression a mix of frustration and skepticism. "Are these all the records?" he pressed.

George, his patience fraying, retorted, "Why would I hide anything?"

I pulled out the photos of Henry and the elusive stranger, presenting them to George. "Have you encountered these two?"

George's response was swift and certain. "No, never seen them."

Beck's fist struck the table in frustration. "Impossible!"

Thinking quickly, I asked, "Are there other places nearby where planes could land?"

George shrugged. "Sure, there's the riverbank and a flat area in the valley. Skilled pilots could manage there."

A flicker of hope reignited. "Do you have records of planes flying overhead?" I asked.

George laughed, incredulous. "You're kidding, right? The skies are busier than the roads. How would I track that?"

Beck closed the record book with a resigned sigh. George, sensing our dejection, asked, "You done?"

With Beck too disheartened to speak, I replied, "Thanks for your help. We're finished here."

George, perhaps seeking some form of solidarity, added, "The woman earlier—she's not my wife, just so you know."

I reassured him, "We're only concerned with our investigation, not your personal matters."

Relieved, George nodded. "Glad to hear it."

As we exited, Beck and I climbed back into the car, the weight of our dead-end search heavy on us. Beck voiced what we both felt. "It's like having a clue that leads nowhere."

I echoed his sentiment, though my mind was already considering alternatives. "The mysterious man likely used a plane, but he wouldn't risk landing at a known airport. Our trail isn't cold yet. We need to backtrack to where he took off."

Beck nodded, a spark of determination reigniting. "Do you think it was Vienna?"

"Even if not Vienna, it can't be far," I reasoned. "That's our next step."

Buoyed by the prospect of a new lead, Beck grinned. "Let's hit the bar. Drinks are on me."

With a renewed sense of purpose, we set off, ready to chase the next thread in our unraveling mystery.

As Beck steered the car into the heart of the city, the neon lights cast a garish glow over Green River City—a place that, despite its small-town reputation, boasted a surprisingly lively bar scene. We parked and entered, the atmosphere inside a stark contrast to the sleepy exterior.

The bar was sprawling, filled with tables and chairs, yet the occupants were mostly sprawled on the floor, a tangled mass of bodies indistinguishable by gender. Their expressions—dazed and euphoric—betrayed the influence of drugs. Some shouted nonsensically, others engaged in languid embraces, while a few mumbled to themselves, all wearing expressions of blissful detachment.

At the counter and scattered among the tables, a few sober—or perhaps merely less intoxicated—patrons sat, their faces etched with melancholy. A record player blared deafening music, and a muted television displayed a speech by some political figure, his silent gesticulations absurdly incongruent with the chaotic revelry around him.

Beck and I navigated the human obstacle course cautiously, though we couldn't avoid stepping on a few limbs in the process. Those we disturbed merely shifted slightly, indifferent to our intrusion. We reached the counter and claimed two seats.

The bartender, busy polishing glasses, eyed us with curiosity. We were clearly outsiders, but Beck's swift order of a bottle of liquor and his impatient gulp seemed to put the bartender at ease. His smile broadened. "New around here?" he asked.

I nodded. "Is that a problem?"

"Not at all," he chuckled. "We just don't cater to the sober. Drunkards are always welcome!"

I managed a wry smile, taking a sip of the potent drink. The bartender leaned in, voice low. "Looking for something a bit more... transformative? Wine can't transport you to the perfect world, you know."

Beck brusquely waved him off. "We're not interested in your mind-altering substances."

Thwarted, the bartender retreated, and we caught the attention of two women down the counter who giggled at our exchange. I sighed, ready to leave, when a commotion drew my attention.

"I swear, I saw them fall from the sky!" an old man with a goatee proclaimed, his beard glistening with spilled wine. His eyes, wide with conviction, scanned the room, challenging the laughter that met his claim.

A middle-aged skeptic retorted, "You drink around the clock. Next, you'll tell us a whole house fell from the sky!"

The old man's voice rose above the din, insistent. "I'm serious! Two people, one just a child. I'm not saying they fell—they had parachutes! The plane went right over me, I heard it, boom boom boom—"

His hands mimicked the motion of a plane soaring overhead, his sound effects drawing more laughter but piquing my interest. I exchanged a look with Beck. Could this be the break we needed in our tangled investigation?

The laughter at the table gradually subsided as the old man continued his earnest tale. "I saw them fall from the sky, two parachutes like white clouds. The young one stood up first. I saw them, but they didn't notice me!"

Beck and I exchanged a knowing glance. This was potentially the breakthrough we needed. I approached the old man, Henry's photo in hand. The conversations around us hushed as I held out the picture. "Is this the boy you saw?"

The old man squinted at the photo, then nodded vigorously. "Yes, that's him!" he exclaimed, leaning in as if to emphasize his point. I gently pushed him back into his chair, stepping away to confer with Beck.

We exited the bar without another word, the gravity of the old man's confirmation hanging between us as we climbed into the car. "It's clear now," Beck said grimly. "Henry is dead."

I nodded, the pieces of the puzzle starting to align. "Yes, he was brought here by that man, parachuting down to avoid detection. It's getting more complicated."

Beck frowned, the implications sinking in. "Arranging a plane and a parachute drop isn't something just anyone can do."

I took a deep breath, the weight of our findings pressing heavily. "We should have seen this coming. We've been shadowing Dr. Connors for a year. His life was no ordinary one."

Beck's eyes met mine, realization dawning. "You think this is the work of an organization?"

"Yes," I replied, the word hanging in the air. "A very tight-knit organization."

Beck's expression turned solemn. "What kind of organization?"

I shook my head, the mystery deepening. "I can't say for sure, but they're clearly monitoring scientists closely."

Beck's smile was bitter, his voice tinged with frustration. "But Dr. Connors committed suicide!"

The contradiction left us both troubled, our path forward shrouded in uncertainty. We drove back to town under a canopy of stars, our minds as dark and tumultuous as the road ahead.

We returned to town at midnight. The next morning, we woke early and retraced our original route.

Beck and I confirmed Henry's death, identifying the mysterious man as his murderer. We linked Henry's death to the films; it seemed Henry had uncovered other secrets as well.

We developed a hypothesis—although Dr. Connors' death appeared to be a suicide, there was a strong sense of a criminal element, possibly involving an organization or group.

We returned to Scientist City by the following afternoon, our thoughts consumed by the shadowy organization we suspected. I parted ways with Beck temporarily; he set off to investigate flight records, while I wandered the city, seeking clarity.

As I meandered through the streets, I found myself near Henry's last known residence, contemplating whether to inform his sister of his fate. Yet, I hesitated, recalling her indifferent demeanor. She seemed detached from her brother's life, and likely his death as well.

Lost in thought, I stood on the sidewalk, the weight of unresolved questions pressing down. It was then I noticed a girl across the street, her eyes fixed on me with an intensity that piqued my curiosity. She couldn't have been more than thirteen, her attire unremarkable, a thick braid trailing down her back.

Feigning disinterest, I continued walking, only to realize she was shadowing my every step. I turned a corner and paused, waiting. Sure enough, she appeared moments later, her pace quickening as she approached.

I moved toward her, cutting off her path. "What do you want to talk to me about?" I asked, my curiosity tempered by the caution that had become second nature.

Chapter 5

The Secret of Henry

The girl stood frozen, eyes wide with a flicker of panic, but her expression shifted as she regained composure. "I hear you've been searching for Henry?"

I nodded, curious. "Yes, who told you?"

"Henry's friends mentioned it. But they don't know the full story," she replied, her voice carrying a hint of mystery. "I'm Henry's best friend."

A surge of interest jolted through me. At their age, a 'best friend' knew all the secrets.

"Then it seems you have some information about Henry," I prompted, my voice steady yet eager.

She hesitated, biting her lower lip before nodding.

The sky above us was deepening into twilight. "How about dinner? We can talk more comfortably," I suggested.

Her eyes lit up. "That's perfect! I've always wanted to try the honey-roasted lamb legs at Maigy Old Store!"

I laughed, nodding in agreement. "Then let's go there."

The famed honey-roasted lamb was indeed a culinary delight, but it paled in comparison to the revelation Lila shared with me over dinner.

"Before he left, Henry confided in me," Lila began, her voice a whisper of urgency. "He said he was heading far away and made me promise not to tell anyone."

I leaned in, ensuring her secrecy was safe with me. "You can trust me."

"Henry met a man," she continued, her expression serious, "a wealthy man who wanted to buy back something he'd lost. Henry refused."

"Why would he turn down money?" I asked, surprised.

Lila's eyes met mine, unwavering. "Henry thought he could get a higher price. The man agreed and took him to get the money. Henry hid the items at a friend's place, saying it was worth tens of thousands. He promised me we could feast on lamb legs every day."

A pang of sorrow gripped me for Henry's naive ambition.

"There was a package," Lila went on, "full of films and a paper with strange lines."

My pulse quickened. In Henry's desk drawer, I'd found such a paper, dismissing it as trivial. How wrong I was!

Lila looked at me and continued, "Henry said he also saw that the man was difficult to deal with. He said that if anything happened to him—"

My heart sank. I wanted to tell her that Henry was dead, but I held back and didn't say it out loud.

Lila's voice lowered further. "Henry overheard the man on the phone. He said if anything happened, the phone number would lead to his assailant."

My heart raced, sensing the weight of this clue. I maintained a calm facade.

"But I promised Henry..." Lila's voice trailed off, eyes downcast.

"You should tell me," I urged gently.

Her lashes fluttered, masking the tears she fought back. "Why? Did something happen to Henry?"

The truth lodged in my throat, too heavy to voice. I remained silent.

"Henry promised to call, no matter what," Lila said, her voice breaking. "But there's been nothing. He must have..."

She looked up, her eyes piercing mine. In that moment, I saw a courage and intelligence far beyond her years.

I nodded, acknowledging the unspoken truth.

A bitter smile played on her lips. "I know Henry's gone. I should tell the police this number."

"You can trust me with it," I insisted. "I'm investigating Henry's death independently. Please believe me."

Lila nodded, quickly scribbling a number with a wet fingertip on the table before erasing it.

Her swift gesture was enough. I had the number committed to memory. Rising from my seat, I noticed Lila's silent tears.

Her grief was raw and genuine, stirring a deep sympathy within me. I reached out, but she spoke first, her voice steady.

"Don't comfort me. I knew this would happen. Henry wanted too much."

Her words stilled my own. I paid the bill, offering her my contact at the hotel should she need anything, then departed Maigy Old Store alone.

Outside, my heart pounded with exhilaration. I had a crucial lead in my quest for the truth.

A phone number, seemingly innocuous, can unravel a web of secrets. As I briskly walked past a phone booth, temptation gnawed at me to dial the number immediately. Yet, a whisper of caution held me back—it might tip off those we were pursuing. First, I needed to pinpoint its origin.

Back at the hotel, my attempts to pry information from the telephone company hit a wall of refusal. I knew I'd have to wait for Beck. Our scheduled call couldn't come soon enough. When it did, urgency colored my voice: "Beck, I need you back here. I've uncovered something crucial."

To my surprise, Beck's response mirrored my own urgency. "I've found something too. Stay put at the hotel."

The line went dead before I could inquire further, leaving me to pace the room in anticipation. Two hours later, the door swung open to reveal Beck, a mix of excitement and triumph in his eyes.

Without preamble, he thrust a piece of paper into my hands—a plane rental record from a small aviation company. The name on the order: Mr. John.

"This has to be our mysterious man," Beck announced, his voice electric with discovery. "The timing and details match perfectly. Look, there's an address."

I studied the paper, skepticism creeping in. "Beck, if I were orchestrating something sinister, I'd never use my real name or address."

He nodded, acknowledging the flaw, yet countered, "True, but it's the only lead we've got."

I offered a thin smile. "I might have something more promising."

As I recounted my encounter with Lila, Beck listened, eyes alight with intrigue. When I finished, he reacted instantly. "We need to trace that phone number's address!"

We left the hotel in a flurry, heading straight for the telephone company. With Beck's credentials, the process unfurled smoothly. Yet, the result left us both staggered.

The registered name and address were there in bold clarity. What caught us off guard was the name—a Japanese one: "Tanaka Maisaichi."

For a moment, we stood speechless, exchanging looks of disbelief. Finally, Beck broke the silence, "Ash, isn't Dr. Tanaka Maisaichi the one who invited you here?"

I grimaced, a bitter smile tugging at my lips. "He did suggest to the Scientist Association to have me come. I can't fathom how this connects—"

The puzzle pieces were scattering in unexpected directions. And somewhere within the chaos, a truth awaited discovery.

Beck's brows knitted into a frown. He remained silent as we stepped out into the drizzle, the rain painting soft patterns on the city streets. As we walked, Beck mused aloud, "If he's involved, it might have been a deliberate move."

I raised an eyebrow, intrigued. "What are you suggesting?"

"He underestimated you," Beck continued, his voice thoughtful. "He believed you'd uncover nothing. By being the one to suggest your invitation, he would naturally deflect suspicion."

His logic was sound. I nodded in agreement. "We need to split up. You gather information on Dr. Tanaka. I'll visit him in person."

Beck hesitated, concern etched on his face. "If he's entangled in this, he could be dangerous. Going alone—"

"I must," I insisted. "Your role is too conspicuous, whereas I'm just a friend. If your hunch is right and he underestimates me, I might glean more from him. Contact me once you have his details."

Reluctantly, Beck shook my hand, and we parted ways. I hailed a streetcar, its wheels splashing through the rain-soaked streets as it carried me to Tanaka Maisaichi's residence.

By the time I arrived, dusk was bleeding into night. I rang the doorbell, the rain now a steady downpour.

A housekeeper answered, her demeanor curt. "Is Dr. Tanaka here? I'm Ash Morris, a friend."

Her expression remained stony as she turned to announce my presence. "Doctor, someone calls for you. It's Ash Morris."

Dr. Tanaka emerged, clad in a traditional kimono and clutching a pipe. Surprise flickered across his features. "Mr. Morris? I thought you had left."

I offered a casual smile. "Seeing me here means I decided to stay."

He didn't press for details, instead gesturing for me to enter. "Come in, make yourself comfortable."

The housekeeper's eyes lingered on me, filled with an unspoken caution, but I brushed it aside and followed Tanaka into his study. It was a room steeped in academia, yet unremarkable. I settled into a chair, noting the subtle tension in his posture as he asked, "How long do you plan to stay?"

I shrugged, feigning nonchalance. "Not sure, really."

Leaning forward, Dr. Tanaka queried, "What brings you here? Anything I can assist with?"

I maintained my smile. "It's about Dr. Connors' death. I can't shake the feeling that something's amiss."

Tanaka's expression betrayed nothing. I continued, "Connors' suicide is beyond doubt. But why was he tailed for a year?"

Tanaka frowned thoughtfully. "That's difficult to explain."

I fixed him with a steady gaze. "I suspect a larger conspiracy."

His dry laughter rang hollow, an attempt to dismiss my notion as fanciful. Yet, beneath the surface, I sensed an undercurrent of anxiety.

"We've initiated a thorough investigation," I continued, "and have gathered some intriguing evidence about these conspiracies."

As I spoke, my eyes never left Tanaka , observing every nuance of his reaction. His fingers twisted together, a classic telltale sign of underlying tension. Though I maintained a facade of composure, I pressed on, "Additionally, we know that poor Henry, the boy who discovered those films and handed them to Professor Anqiaojia, has been found dead."

Tanaka 's shock was palpable. It wasn't just the news of Henry's demise that shook him—it was the realization that I was aware of it. If Tanaka had any involvement, the meticulous orchestration of Henry's death, disguised as an accident miles away, should have remained a secret. My revelation pierced that illusion, and his shock seemed almost inevitable.

"Henry is dead?" Tanaka stammered, his voice fraught with disbelief. "Who would murder a child?"

I seized the moment, my tone sharp as I leaned forward. "Dr. Tanaka, I only mentioned Henry's death. How did you know it was murder?"

This was a classic trap, a maneuver to catch an accomplice off guard, often seen in detective novels. If he were complicit, his immediate reaction would be telling. Yet, Tanaka only hesitated briefly before replying, "You mentioned conspiracies, implying foul play, so I assumed Henry was killed."

His explanation flowed naturally, a plausible defense. Yet I remained skeptical. My instincts and the evidence I had gathered led me here, so I wasn't inclined to accept his words so readily. I let out a dry chuckle, "We've identified a mysterious figure who visited Connors on the eve of his death. Connors left with him, and the man vanished thereafter."

Tanaka shifted uneasily in his seat. "I recall that—didn't you show me the sketch of the mysterious man?"

"Exactly," I replied, my voice steady and sure. "And I am convinced this man is Henry's murderer."

Tanaka's eyes widened, a low gasp escaping his lips.

I leaned in, my gaze piercing, relentless. "Who is this mysterious man?"

The reaction from Dr. Tanaka was immediate and more intense than I had anticipated. As we sat face to face, the color drained from his face, leaving it ghostly pale. His eyes widened with a mixture of fear and desperation.

Before I could fully process his response, he let out a strange cry. His hand moved with a speed and precision that betrayed his mastery of karate—a skill I had not associated with him, a man of intellect and science. His hand shot forward, fingers curled in a classic karate posture, and before I could react, his edge-of-the-hand strike landed squarely on my neck.

Pain exploded, and my vision blurred with stars as I struggled to stay conscious. The force of the blow sent me tumbling backward, chair and all, crashing to the floor. Helplessly, I lay there, my body refusing to obey the commands to rise.

Tanaka was on his feet in an instant. He stepped over, and his foot came down hard on my head, a brutal follow-up designed to incapacitate. The world swam around me, and I fought to hold onto consciousness, the training I'd undergone keeping me from slipping completely into the void.

Despite the pain, instinct kicked in. I reached out blindly, my hand catching his calf as his foot lifted briefly off my head. It was a weak move, but it was all I could muster. My grip was tenuous, fueled more by desperation than strength, but it was enough to unbalance him slightly, causing him to stagger.

CHAPTER 6

THE UNSOLVABLE CONTRADICTION

The leverage I had on Tanaka Maisaichi sent him tumbling forward. His cry was sharp, and he fell to the ground with a thud. As he hit the floor, I rubbed my neck, trying to regain my senses. My vision was still blurred, and the room spun slightly around me.

I heard a series of crashes echo from the living room. When I finally managed to stand, albeit unsteadily, I noticed several items had been knocked over in his frantic escape. The housekeeper appeared at the doorway, her face a mask of panic. "What's going on?" she demanded.

Breathing heavily, I croaked out, "Where is Dr. Tanaka?"

Before she could respond, a gunshot shattered the air, reverberating through the house.

Instinct took over. "Call the police!" I shouted, my voice raw. I surged toward the source of the sound, but the earlier blows had taken their toll, and I stumbled, collapsing to the ground once more.

"The gunshot came from the doctor's room!" the housekeeper cried.

Fueled by adrenaline, I forced myself upright, yelling again, "Call the police!" Using the wall for support, I staggered forward, navigating the hallway until I reached a closed door. I rammed it with my shoulder, and on the fourth attempt, it gave way with a splintering crash.

Inside, the scene was grim. Tanaka Maisaichi lay on the bed, a gun in his hand, smoke curling lazily from the barrel. Blood pooled around him, stark against the sheets. The bullet had pierced his temple, the close range leaving a gruesome scene I could barely stand to witness.

Despite the open windows, the reality was clear: Dr. Tanaka Masaichi had taken his own life.

I stood frozen at the threshold, unable to tear my eyes from the horror before me. My mind churned with questions, the foremost being about the mysterious man and the motive behind Tanaka's drastic action. Had fear of exposure driven him to this end? Was he complicit in the deaths of Henry and Dr. Connors?

The weight of these questions bore down on me, with no immediate answers in sight. Tanaka's death left a tangled web of intrigue and secrets, and I was determined to unravel it, no matter how deep I had to go. But was this suicide a confession of guilt or an act of desperation? The truth remained elusive, buried beneath layers of deceit.

I stood at the door, lost in thought, until the distant whir of a police siren jolted me back to reality. The sound grew louder, signaling the arrival of law enforcement. As I turned, holding onto the door frame for support, two officers approached me swiftly.

Without hesitation, they took in the grim scene of Tanaka Maisaichi's body and grabbed my arm, twisting it behind my back. I offered no resistance; I knew the truth would soon surface.

More officers arrived, filling the room with a tense energy. I was led to the living room, where a senior officer soon entered and assessed the situation. "Let him go," he instructed. "The deceased committed suicide."

The officers released their grip, though skepticism lingered in their eyes. My voice was weary as I addressed them. "Verify my identity with the National Security Bureau—special investigator, Beck Bice. This case should fall under their jurisdiction."

"Perhaps," one officer replied, "but you'll need to accompany us to the station for now."

Exhaustion weighed heavily on me, and I simply nodded, resigned to the process. At the station, I was left alone in a stark room. Two hours passed before Beck strode in, his presence a welcome sight.

He pulled up a chair and sat opposite me, joined by two senior officers. "They mentioned you were uncooperative," Beck said, a hint of amusement in his voice.

I managed a wry smile. "They didn't have the full picture. I'm glad you're here. Here's what happened−" I recounted my encounter with Tanaka Maisaichi in detail, leaving nothing out.

Beck listened intently, his brow furrowed. Once I finished, he turned to the officers, then back to me, patting my shoulder. "You're clear. Tanaka clearly took his own life out of fear."

His certainty was reassuring, and I knew he must have solid evidence. I looked at him expectantly.

"I contacted the General Administration," Beck explained. "They have a file on Tanaka. It reveals he spent time in Hokkaido during his college years, disappearing sporadically. I believe he was traveling to Sakhalin Island."

The implication hit me. "Not exactly a tourist destination. He was likely receiving training there—a spy."

Beck nodded. "Exactly. The mysterious man and Tanaka were likely accomplices in Henry's murder. Your questions probably made him panic."

He paused, then added, "For those trained as he was, exposure often leads to only one exit—suicide."

I sighed, rising slowly. "I believe you're right. His karate skills were formidable enough; he nearly broke my neck."

One of the officers acknowledged with a nod. "You can leave now."

Relieved yet reflective, I stepped out, pondering the tangled web of deceit and desperation that had led us here. There was still much to uncover, and I was determined to see it through.

Beck advised, "We should keep the details from the press. We'll manage the situation internally." The officers agreed, and soon Beck and I were in his car, leaving the station behind.

He paused before starting the engine, turning to me with a serious expression, "Ash, this situation keeps getting more tangled."

But I disagreed, "On the contrary, it's starting to unravel."

Beck's skepticism was evident. I explained, "Only a significant organization could maintain surveillance on Dr. Connors for an entire year, which suggests we're dealing with more than just a lone actor."

"But Connors committed suicide," Beck pointed out.

"Then why the urgency to recover the films if they were inconsequential?" I countered.

Beck pondered silently, the implications dawning. "And remember," I continued, "the mysterious man's identity aligns with Tanaka Maisaichi. Before Connors' death, he met this man. The key lies in understanding their conversation and where they went."

Beck nodded thoughtfully. "Perhaps the mysterious man attempted to sway Connors, offering a deal. Maybe Connors initially accepted but later regretted it, leading to his suicide."

I frowned. "We shouldn't tarnish Connors' reputation posthumously."

"My theory is plausible," Beck defended.

But I shook my head. "Connors' behavior, as seen in his documentaries, was beyond reproach. He wouldn't have left himself vulnerable to coercion. Why would he betray his principles?"

"Then why did he end his life?" Beck pressed.

"I don't know yet," I admitted. "But now that we have a lead on the mysterious man's identity, finding him is within reach."

"Absolutely," Beck agreed, starting the car and driving me back to the hotel.

That night, I lay awake, piecing together the puzzle in my mind. Lila's involvement had led me to Tanaka Maisaichi's phone number, and from there, clarity emerged from the chaos.

Dr. Connors' research had the potential for military application, a tempting target for international espionage. Tanaka's duplicitous nature wasn't unexpected, given the stakes. Even acquaintances of many years can conceal their true selves.

Yet, one question persisted: Why did Dr. Connors die?

The investigation felt cyclical, returning to its origins.

The puzzle gnawed at me: if the films of Dr. Connors' activities bore no criminal intent, their loss should have been inconsequential. Yet, the murderer went to great lengths to retrieve them, culminating in Henry's death. This suggested the films held damning evidence or a secret too dangerous to be exposed.

The murderer's desperation to recover the films pointed to a deeper conspiracy. Perhaps they feared Henry's disappearance would draw too much attention, or maybe they hoped Professor Anqiaojia, buried under his mountain of work, would overlook the package Henry had entrusted to him. This oversight would offer them the perfect opportunity to retrieve it. However, curiosity got the better of Anqiaojia. He viewed the films, inadvertently throwing a wrench into the murderer's meticulously laid plans.

Once the films were seen by many, retrieving them became futile. Thus, Tanaka Maisaichi's involvement in inviting me for the investigation seemed like a miscalculated risk. He underestimated my capabilities, likely expecting me to be a bumbling detective who'd leave empty-handed.

His misjudgment was nearly realized; if not for Beck's intervention at the airport, I might have departed without uncovering anything substantial. Ironically, Tanaka's invitation sealed his fate, leading to his downfall.

The recording of Dr. Connors' actions indeed suggested a nefarious intent. The mysterious man's direct interaction with Connors implied they had sinister plans. Yet Connors' suicide remained an enigma, a contradiction that stymied progress and trapped the investigation in a loop.

Despite the evidence of Connors' suicide being irrefutable, the case seemed at a dead end, frustratingly going in circles.

The following day at noon, Beck arrived at the hotel with palpable excitement. His enthusiasm was infectious as he announced, "We found him!"

Having worked closely with Beck, I understood immediately that he referred to the mysterious man. His revelation electrified me. "That's excellent news! Have you detained him? Let's go see him!" I urged.

Beck hesitated, looking slightly embarrassed. "Not quite. I've identified him, but haven't seen him in person. However, I've arranged for a temporary blockade of the area where he's located."

While it wasn't the complete resolution I hoped for, it was a significant step forward. The identity of the mysterious man could unlock the secrets that had eluded us, and I was eager to follow this lead to its conclusion.

Beck's explanation left me puzzled at first, but as he elaborated, understanding dawned. "That's right," he continued. "We know this mysterious man's identity as a spy. They often use diplomatic cover. I discovered he's Rudaf, listed as a second assistant in news photography at the consulate. Doesn't that sound odd?"

"Not at all," I replied. "He likely organized the filming. Rudaf must be quite the photography expert. Did you attempt to meet him at the consulate?"

Beck nodded. "I did, but they claimed he had returned home. I was skeptical, so I checked the departure records. Sure enough, he left."

I acknowledged this with a "Hmm," and then asked, "But you mentioned a location was blocked. What does that entail?"

Beck explained, "I tracked Rudaf's activities and found he owned a small house in the northern suburbs. With a prosecutor's order, local police have sealed it off. Let's go there; we might uncover something."

Despite his excitement, I couldn't help but yawn. Beck looked surprised at my reaction. I patted his shoulder, saying, "A seasoned spy like him wouldn't leave anything behind. Since he's gone, I'm inclined to head back."

Beck pleaded, "It's worth a look. We might discover something."

Knowing Beck's persistence, I relented. "Alright, let's check it out."

He helped with my coat, and we headed downstairs to his car, driving towards the northern suburbs. During the drive, we exchanged thoughts, agreeing that Dr. Connors' suicide might be linked to his meeting with Rudaf. But the nature of their conversation remained elusive.

Upon arrival, a police officer greeted us. I surveyed the small brick house, noting its garden and the similar house nearby. The secluded setting seemed a prudent choice for someone like Rudaf.

The officer shook hands with Beck and reported, "Witnesses saw Rudaf and another man here. It resembled Dr. Connors."

Beck was taken aback. "Was it that day?"

The officer replied, "The exact date escapes witnesses, but it was close to Dr. Connors' suicide."

Beck turned to me, and I confirmed, "Yes, it was the day before."

The officer eyed me curiously, so I elaborated, "Rudaf visited Connors, who left with him. The housekeeper noted Connors was gone for some time before returning alone. Rudaf brought him here."

"What transpired here?" Beck murmured as we approached the house.

Inside, the space was deserted, with disarray hinting at a hurried departure. We searched quickly but found nothing overtly suspicious. Beck collected paper scraps near an old desk, hoping for clues.

Meanwhile, I noticed an unusual aquarium beneath a window. It was a two-foot-by-two-foot tank, typically for tropical fish, but filled with soil instead of water. A dense wire mesh covered it. Intrigued, I squatted to inspect further and saw small bumblebees busily burrowing in the soil.

Their presence was curious, and I wondered if they held any significance to Rudaf's activities or the broader mystery at hand. As Beck sifted through the paper scraps, I pondered the possible connection, aware that even the smallest detail could unlock new insights into this tangled affair.

The presence of the round-flowered bumblebee in the home of a spy like Rudaf was certainly unusual. As I squatted down to observe the bees, Beck joined me, curious about my focus. I pointed to the aquarium, noting the peculiarity of keeping such bees unless Rudaf had a specific purpose, like filming a documentary about them.

Beck considered this and suddenly exclaimed, "I found the murderer of Dr. Connors!" His outburst startled me. He pointed at the bees, suggesting they were the culprits, perhaps due to an allergy Connors had. I sighed, recognizing his leap of logic. "Beck, you should be writing novels. Connors died from drug poisoning, verified by his own purchase."

Beck blinked, realizing his error, and sighed. "So, what's the use of Rudaf keeping these bumblebees?"

I shrugged. "It could be a hobby. People have peculiar interests. I know someone who enjoys befriending fleas."

Beck chuckled, "Don't joke!"

"I'm serious, Beck. Anyway, I'm leaving tomorrow."

Beck stood, clapping his hands in resignation. "Alright, I guess there's nothing more here."

We watched the ongoing search, aware that the likelihood of finding anything was slim. After four hours, we left for the city. That evening, Beck visited me, holding a piece of paper reconstructed from scraps found in Rudaf's trash. It was an incomplete picture but mostly pieced together, filled with irregular, chaotic lines.

Beck spread it out before me, asking if it held any significance. I pondered silently, remembering a similar image I'd seen at Henry's.

"Yes," I acknowledged. "Henry had something like this. It seemed meaningless, just repetitive lines. The Scientist Association had seen it, and Lila mentioned it too."

Beck inquired if the two images were the same. "Not identical, but similar in their chaotic nature," I replied, raising my gaze. "Do you think there's a hidden meaning?"

Beck sighed. "It's hard to say. I won't keep you from leaving, but let's stay in touch."

CHAPTER 7

SUICIDE OR MURDER?

"Of course, I'll give you my phone number. You should contact me, and the long-distance call fee can be billed to the agency account. If I were to contact you, the cost would be too high!" Beck laughed and punched me on the shoulder, and I reciprocated with a respectful punch. We clapped hands, but he didn't accompany me to the airport. His demeanor suggested he was eager to uncover the secret in the picture, though I doubted there was any hidden meaning in those chaotic lines.

The next day, I returned home. The trip had been unpleasant, but being home brought a sense of relaxation.

Flora blamed me, arguing that I should have returned long ago after confirming Dr. Connors' suicide. I didn't argue, simply recounting the events as they had unfolded.

Beck never contacted me after I got home, and gradually, I left this journey behind.

Several months later, I arranged to meet a friend at a bar at 2 pm.

Arriving a few minutes early, I was stunned when I saw Beck! For a moment, I doubted my own eyes. Beck's presence wasn't impossible, but he should have contacted me if he had come.

The dim bar lights obscured my view, but as I looked closer, I confirmed the young man was indeed, the special investigator.

However, something extremely serious must have happened to him, as his demeanor was shocking. Simply put, at this moment, Beck was a drunkard. No other term fit someone drinking this heavily in the afternoon.

He sat alone at a table, a bottle of wine and a glass in front of him. Leaning forward, he fiddled with something on the table, but the dark light made it difficult to see.

As I approached, my surprise grew. He hadn't shaved in weeks, and his hair was messy—completely different from the energetic young man I once knew.

Afraid I had the wrong person, I didn't call his name but coughed loudly to get his attention. I expected him to look up and recognize me, avoiding any awkwardness.

But he seemed deaf to my cough, maintaining his posture, eyes fixed on the table.

When I looked at the table, I was stunned. Crawling on it was a beetle.

As I sat across from him, his attention remained fixed on the scarab beetle crawling on the table, seemingly oblivious to my presence.

The scarab beetle, with its golden green hard shell, is a fascinating insect often given as a gift to children. But Beck was no longer a child. Yet, in his current state, he seemed entirely absorbed by the crawling beetle, as if nothing else in the world deserved his attention.

I couldn't help it after seeing this, so I coughed again and shouted loudly, "Beck!"

Beck's body shook slightly at my shout, and he looked up at me. I immediately put on a smile like an old friend reunited.

However, I quickly realized my smile was in vain. Beck seemed not to recognize me at all. He just glanced at me and then lowered his head again. In that brief moment, I saw a deep sadness on his face.

When he raised his head, I was even more certain it was Beck. Despite him lowering his head again, I sat down opposite him. "Beck, what happened?"

Beck didn't answer, still staring at the beetle, which made me a little angry. I flicked the beetle off the table, sending it flying to the ground, and shouted again, "Beck, what happened? If you don't tell me, I'll punch your front teeth out!"

Beck didn't answer me at first; he simply picked up the wine glass and drank half of its contents in one gulp. He then reached for the bottle to pour more, but I grabbed it, stopping him. "Beck, that's enough. When did you become a drunkard?"

Finally, Beck spoke. It was only then that I confirmed I had not mistaken his identity. His voice was unnervingly calm. "Let me drink, Ash."

"No, not until I understand what happened to you. I want to keep you sober enough to tell me what's going on," I replied.

Beck hesitated, his hand retracting from the bottle. He rubbed his face repeatedly, revealing the weight of his heavy mental burden.

"Beck," I repeated, my tone softening. "Talk to me. What's going on?"

He relented, setting the bottle down, and began to recount the events. "Do you still remember Rudaf?" he asked.

"Of course," I replied. Rudaf was unforgettable—the mysterious man linked to Dr. Connors and Henry's deaths.

Beck continued, "After you left, I submitted our report, and it seemed like the case was closed. But about half a month ago, I got a notice from my superiors. They had traced Rudaf to a Southeast Asian country, still posing as a diplomat."

I was taken aback. "He dared to surface again?"

"Yes," Beck said, remaining still. "My superiors asked for my input. I expressed a strong desire to meet this so-called second-level photography assistant, and I was deployed."

"Why didn't you contact me?" I asked, puzzled.

He paused, then explained, "Once I left our country, my mission was classified. My superiors didn't want to draw extra attention to my movements."

I nodded, understanding the need for secrecy. "So, did you finally meet Rudaf?"

Beck nodded but hesitated to elaborate further. His silence spoke volumes, suggesting the encounter had been significant, perhaps even traumatic. I waited patiently, sensing he needed time to process before he could share more.

At this point, I was eager to know how he met Rudaf, but seeing how tired he was, I couldn't bear to rush him.

After a while, Beck suddenly laughed, a helpless smile. "Do you remember the jar of bumblebees in Rudaf's hut?"

I raised an eyebrow, "I remember."

Beck continued, "I said at the time that those bumblebees were murderers, and you laughed at me for talking nonsense!"

I was extremely surprised, but I didn't say anything. I was just thinking, what did Beck mean by saying this? Dr. Connors committed suicide; his death couldn't possibly be related to that jar of bumblebees.

Beck went on, "Of course, the jar of bumblebees can't be considered the murderer, but as an accomplice—"

I couldn't help but interrupt, "Beck, can you tell the story from the beginning?"

He rolled his eyes and looked at me, "Okay. I met Rudaf. He naturally didn't know who I was, so I used a little trick, the usual trick spies use, to take him to a secluded place. This guy got scared and told me everything."

I asked quickly, "What did he say?"

Beck said, "Rudaf said their plan was to bribe Dr. Connors, and if that didn't work, they would kill him."

I nodded, understanding the gravity of what he was saying. "The bribe didn't work, did it?"

"No, it didn't," Beck confirmed. "When all attempts failed, they moved to plan B—murder. And, tragically, they succeeded."

"But Connors committed suicide," I countered, trying to reconcile this with the official reports.

Beck continued, unfazed by my interjection. "Their plan was insidious, crafted with the input of a renowned psychologist. This psychologist devised a strategy that played on Connors' mind."

"A psychologist?" I echoed, bewildered.

"Yes," Beck affirmed, taking another sip of his drink. "This psychologist was a master manipulator, someone who could see into the depths of a person's psyche."

He paused, resting his head on the table, and I urged him to continue. After a moment, he lifted his head and explained, "They had professionals shadow Connors for a year, documenting his every move outside. They learned his habits, his routines."

"But how could that lead to murder?" I asked, still grappling with the implications.

Beck glanced at me, and I was stunned. His eyes, usually brimming with vitality, were now filled with disappointment and dejection. It was a look that shouldn't belong to someone so young and full of life.

Beck's story unraveled a sinister scheme that went beyond conventional means of manipulation. As he continued, the depth of the psychological trap set for Dr. Connors became increasingly clear.

"You've seen those documentary films," Beck reiterated, his voice tinged with bitterness. "Dr. Connors's life looked normal, like anyone else's."

"Yes, what's wrong with that?" I asked, still trying to connect the dots.

Beck explained how the repeated lines on paper mapped Connors' movements over the past year, a visual depiction of his life's patterns. These lines, seemingly innocuous, were used to illustrate the monotony and predictability of his routine.

"By showing Connors these lines and the documentaries, they highlighted the ordinariness of his life," Beck said. "He probably denied understanding the significance, which led to the pivotal part of their plan."

I listened intently, refraining from interrupting, knowing Beck needed to tell the story in his own time.

Beck took another sip of wine. "Do you remember that box of bumblebees?"

I nodded. "You've asked me before. I remember."

Beck's voice dropped, becoming even more somber. "The murderer—" He paused. I knew exactly who he meant, so I just nodded.

"The murderer took out a bumblebee and placed it on a piece of white paper. This type of bumblebee is a digging bee. Like all insects, their actions are programmed. From larvae to adults, their behavior is instinctual. There are codes in their chromosomes, similar to the components in a computer. Each part has a fixed function, governed by preset rules that never change."

I listened intently, finding Beck's explanation complex yet comprehensible. However, I couldn't yet grasp why he was saying all this.

Beck continued, "Before laying eggs, these bumblebees dig a hole in the ground, then searches for a caterpillar. After finding one, it inspects the hole, catch the caterpillar, and drag it into the hole headfirst. If you move the caterpillar away while it's inspecting the hole, what do you think will happen?"

I was momentarily stunned. "It will go find the caterpillar!"

Beck laughed. "No, it will repeat the same action of dragging the caterpillar, regardless of where it is. Move it once, it'll do it again. Move it ten times, it'll do it ten times. This is encoded in its life."

I took a deep breath, still struggling to understand the significance of the bumblebee's behavior.

Beck shook his wine glass. ""The murderers used the bumblebees to demonstrate a point," Beck continued. "They placed a bumblebee on paper, making it perform its instinctual actions. It left marks similar to Connors' activity tracks. They then showed Connors these marks, alongside his own, without saying a word, just laughing. That laughter was the final blow." Beck clenched his right fist and knocked hard on the table. "At that moment, the murderer's goal was achieved. Dr. Connors committed suicide the next day!"

The image of Connors, a man of intellect, being reduced to despair by such a cruel comparison, was haunting. The murderers had used psychological warfare, convincing Connors that his life was as predetermined and insignificant as that of an insect.

I took a slow breath, feeling a sudden dizziness. After a long pause, realization hit me. "They wanted him to believe his life was no different than a bumblebee's, following a repetitive, meaningless pattern."

Beck raised his head. "Exactly. Dr. Connors was a high-level intellectual, believing that humans are the masters of the earth, capable of achieving anything through effort. But suddenly, he realized that the so-called master of all things was no different from insects. Just imagine, how could he still be interested in living?"

"No interest in living," was a phrase I had never heard before, but I believed without reservation that Dr. Connors had committed suicide under such circumstances.

The weight of Beck's words hung heavily in the air, resonating with a bleak sense of existential despair. The comparison of his own life to that of an insect was a stark reflection of the psychological impact the investigation had had on him. It was as if the realization of life's perceived monotony and predetermined patterns had seeped into his own consciousness, mirroring the fate that had befallen Dr. Connors.

I was stunned for a long time before I said, "So that's the case. Then what happened to you?"

Beck looked at me straight, then leaned over, fumbled on the ground for a while, and caught the beetle. He placed it on the table, letting it crawl slowly. "Me? What do you want me to do? My life is the same as that of insects. I just live like an insect!"

I took a breath. "You often travel thousands of miles, and your life is wide-ranging—"

Beck immediately interrupted, "Even if I travel every day, even if I often travel between major planets, my activities can still be drawn into a regular track, a regular line determined by the genetic code. This is my life. What do you think is the meaning?"His question about the meaning of it all was profound, one that philosophers and thinkers have grappled with for centuries.

"You—you're out there, traveling, experiencing so much," I tried to counter, but his retort was immediate and poignant.

"Even with all that, my life still follows a track," he insisted. "No matter where I go, it's all part of a predetermined path. What's the point?"

His words struck a chord within me, reflecting an existential crisis that many face when confronted with the notion of determinism versus free will. The idea that life, in all its complexity, might be reduced to simple patterns was a sobering thought.

I took a swig from the bottle, feeling the burn of the liquor as it coursed through me, offering a temporary escape from the weight of such thoughts. In that moment, I understood the allure of numbing oneself to the harsh realities of existence, the same allure that led many down the path of alcohol or other vices.

As the pieces of the puzzle fell into place, a realization dawned on me—a revelation as profound as any ancient secret unearthed in the catacombs of history. In this city, with its labyrinthine streets and shadowed alleys, the air thrummed with the echoes of a timeless question. It became clear why the taverns overflowed with those seeking solace in a bottle, why the sweet, smoky tendrils of marijuana wove their way through the night, and why the intellectual elite wrestled with the very fabric of existence.

Insects, those tiny architects of instinct, never pause to contemplate their existence; they march to the rhythm of an unchanging pattern, nature's clockwork soldiers. Likewise, the unthinking masses drift through life, blind to the deeper currents that swirl around them, content to follow the well-trodden paths laid before them.

Yet, those who dared to peer beyond the veil of the ordinary—those possessed by the fire of knowledge—found themselves ensnared in a web of existential inquiry. They pondered the ultimate enigma: What distinguishes our lives from the mechanical dance of insects?

In this city, where the past and present converged in a tapestry of science, history, and faith, the search for meaning became a quest as ancient as time itself. And I found myself drawn into the mystery, compelled to seek my own answers in the intricate mosaic of human existence.

The more we ponder the meaning of life, the more elusive it can seem, especially when faced with the notion that our lives might mirror the simplicity of an insect's existence. Yet, in that simplicity, there is also a kind of beauty—an acceptance of life's rhythms and cycles.

As the alcohol dulled my senses, I felt myself drifting away from the complexity of these thoughts. I no longer knew if my friend had arrived, nor did it seem to matter.

In that haze, I found a strange sense of peace, a temporary suspension of the existential questions that had loomed so large.

In that moment, I realized that while the search for meaning is a deeply human endeavor, sometimes it's okay to let go, to simply be, and to find solace in the understanding that life's value isn't solely defined by its complexity or predictability, but by the connections we make and the moments we share.

EPILOGUE

In the heart of the bustling metropolis, where the pulse of humanity beats with relentless precision, lies a truth often overlooked: our lives, when meticulously charted, mirror the intricate patterns of insects. The story I weave is not one of despair, nor does it whisper the dark allure of escape through finality. Instead, it unveils an undeniable revelation.

Within the labyrinthine stretches of concrete and steel, our existence unfolds within ten-mile confines. Our travels, though they seem expansive, are but extensions of our daily paths.

Yet, within this seeming constraint, our minds possess an immeasurable freedom, capable of soaring beyond the earthly shackles, into the heavens, through the earth's core, and across the vast tapestry of the cosmos that stretches billions of light years away.

This boundless capacity for thought might indeed be the very essence of our survival.

Amidst the hum of the city, have we, like insects, grown comfortable within our routine? Perhaps it is only those with profound wisdom who discern the melancholy undertones and the elusive search for meaning.

These reflections, though profound, extend beyond the boundaries of this narrative.

Here, in the intricate dance of science, history, and the whispers of the divine, lies a puzzle waiting to be unraveled.